The Bright Report

Volume 1

MARCEL M DU PLESSIS

Copyright © 2021 Marcel Masuret Du Plessis

All rights reserved.

ISBN: 979-8-5764-7888-0

Cover design by the author (using Canva)

The following is a work of fiction. Any resemblance to persons living or dead is purely coincidental. The Timely Journal's stories are not as good as these, even if they are 'truer'.

DEDICATION

To those who kitjovistinope,
and keep trying…

CONTENTS

	Acknowledgments	i
Art:	Kitjovistinope	1
Literature:	The Chiprock Recluse	9
Sport:	The Derby	23
Travel:	People of the Cloud	31
Motoring:	Reviewing the Lethe Series D	39
Entertainment:	A Boardgame Story	61
Editor's Note:	Meet the Staff	73
	Extras	77
	About the Author	83
	Other Titles by the Author	85

ACKNOWLEDGMENTS

Special thanks to my Mother for two reasons: firstly, for having a dream wherein I invented a word for "a row of kittens jumping rope" – without you I would not have the inspiration for the first story in this collection; secondly, for imbuing me with an ethos of hard work and persistence.

I would like to thank my Dad who has always suggested that independent publishing is the way to go – here's hoping Dad!

I thank every friend and acquaintance that has given me a word of encouragement or constructive criticism. I am the sum of all the people I have met and a product of their love – I hope you know who you are.

Lastly, I thank you, the reader. Thank you for taking a chance on a book and an author you have never heard of. I hope that you find joy, laughter, and meaning in the words you are about to read and that you will do so again in future.

ART: KITJOVISTINOPE
BY PASH TENSING

Kitjovistinope. Enigma. Cultural sensation. The word has taken the world by storm, but where did it come from? What does it even mean?

It is this reporter's wish to answer these questions and – by extension – get to the bottom of the issue of hopeless endeavors.

But, before we get to the business of definitions, it is important to understand where this *Kitjovistinope* business started.

This brings us to number Forty-Seven Ramshackle Lane, the home of Mr and Mrs Krinkle. An ordinary home by all accounts: white picket fence, double garage with room for a tandem, and a four-story house – most rooms unused. The lawn was immaculate – Mrs Krinkle saw to it that each blade was exactly forty-seven millimeters long. Each picket was *Moore's Egg White number fifteen*. Each bush and tree had an odd number of leaves, and there were exactly forty-seven steppingstones leading from the French windows to a non-functioning, yet decorative, fountain.

Mrs Krinkle liked things to be neat.

She worked at *Vonnegut's Candle and Lamp Manufacturing Co.* as Under-Deputy Candle Appraiser and Keeper of the Tape Measure. She was proud of her career and was looking forward to being promoted to Over-Deputy Candle Appraiser. She was even trusted with the security of the office tape measure – locked securely in the home safe behind the painting entitled *Austere Landscape number seven*.

Mrs Krinkle was the picture of neatness. She even arranged the threatening letters (written in untidy, wobbly script) from Mrs Bradshaw (resident of number Forty-Nine Ramshackle Lane) in a neat pile by the door – exactly three centimeters from the key bowl, which was empty, of course. Mrs Krinkle would not allow something as disorderly as a bowl of keys. Neat – orderly – organized – that was Mrs Krinkle.

Mr Krinkle was not neat. Mr Krinkle was chaos personified, for he was an artist. *Austere Landscapes* (numbers one through thirteen) were not the product of his brush. Not since an early work entitled *Family Walk in Park* did the subjects of Mr Krinkle's paintings include things such as landscapes (e.g. parks), people (e.g. families), or objects (e.g. strollers).

Mr Krinkle lived in the chaotic world of the abstract. No brushstroke was ever the same width or length or shared the same intent. His works were messy and – in the words of Dunken B. Farnsburrow, chief art critic of *Snub Magazine* – "Hard to take seriously".

He worked in a small room on the ground level that was not entirely suited to the function of "*Studio*". In fact, the room was labelled "*Nursery*" in the original building plans. But Mr. Krinkle made it work. He spent nine hours a day splashing paint onto canvas – taking the occasional break to perform meditative cussing. This rigorous work-ethic led to a body of paintings numbering in the thousands.

Despite eager buyers in the form of motel owners, open-minded collectors, and the world of competitive interior decorating, Mr Krinkle struggled to make a name for himself. There were several well-attended exhibitions over the years, but no matter how colorful the pamphlets or how impressive the paintings, Mr Krinkle failed to embed his name in the collective conscious of the art world.

I am sure that even you, dear loyal reader of the Bright Report, struggle to place the name Worbal Krinkle. But say now that you are cured of this ignorance, for it is said Worbal Krinkle who brought *Kitjovistinope* to the world.

It all started on a frantic Wednesday afternoon at forty-seven minutes past three. Mrs Krinkle arrived home from the candle factory and triple checked that the tape measure was in her purse. She also made sure that her economy car was parked exactly, that the garage was shut precisely, and that the stones from the walkway to the front door were aligned. She gave an appraising glance to the hydrangea by the front door – there was an even number of baby blue flowering heads – she would have to address this.

But on this particular Wednesday, gardening had to wait. For all was not well at number Forty-Seven Ramshackle Lane. There was a pile of canvases next to the bin. Mrs Krinkle was so distracted by the *Hydrangea macrophylla* that she almost knocked the disorderly tower over. She realized that "canvases" was not an entirely apt description. The canvases were covered in paint – the bulk of Mr Krinkle's "*Swirly Mauve Contemplation*" collection. Not canvases – paintings.

She neatened up the pile slightly, straightened her pencil skirt, sighed, and unlocked the door. What she witnessed within she later described to this reporter as "*shockingly untidy*". The paint-stained contents of his Studio were usually – much to the content of Mrs Krinkle – limited to the only room in the house she did not care for. But on this historically charged afternoon, the barrier between neatness and chaos had ruptured. Brushes, pallet knives, greasy bottles of linseed oil and turpentine, easels, paintings – half-finished, finished, scrapped, and never-started – spilled into the hallway like the beachfront after the sinking of a container ship.

While the lady herself denies this, several neighbors heard her scream at fifty-one minutes past three. They also report that the screaming stopped at approximately fifty-five minutes past three. The accuracy of this fact is in dispute and entirely extraneous.

Mr Krinkle had emptied the Studio. Gone were the projects and tools of yesterday. Abandoned was his "*Mauve Contemplation*" project. While some of us – this journalist included – would balk at the idea of throwing out everything and starting from scratch, Mr Krinkle's soul had been lit by the proverbial fire of inspiration.

Mrs Krinkle crept into the room with the caution of a bomb-disposal team taking their first steps into the red zone. She discovered that an entire wall of the cramped room had been repainted in *Hopeful Chalkboard Black number four*. She found Mr Krinkle staring at it – his hands were stained like those of a bird rescuer after an oil spill. In the center of the black void on the newly painted surface was a trickle of white – a single runny word.

Mrs Krinkle sounded it out: KIT-JO-VIS-TI-NOPE.

She told this humble reporter that her utterance seemed to rouse her husband from his stupor. He turned to her and said: "I've done it, Jane. I've found something new. I've invented a new word."

He then went on to define it for Mrs Krinkle. Needless to say, she was not impressed by the original meaning of the word. In fact, when she recounted the events of this afternoon to me, she seemed more concerned about the mess in the hallway than this momentous discovery.

Mr Krinkle was convinced about the importance of the word the moment it came to him. "This was it. I knew it. When I painted the word, I knew it would be big. If only I knew just how big it would get!"

"He was inconsolable," said Mrs Krinkle. "He didn't care about his other work – or the fact that they were making the rest of the house untidy. It was just the word – that's all that mattered."

Shortly after revealing the word to Mrs Krinkle, Mr Krinkle decided to invest in silkscreen equipment. "T-shirts! I knew it had to be T-shirts!"

This, as it turned out, was the moment that it all took off. The shirts sold out. And so did the next run and the run after that. Kitjovistinope escaped into the world and lodged itself firmly into the public consciousness.

Against all odds, the nonsense took off. This jumble of letters appealed to people from all over the world – young and old; rich and poor; art lovers and art haters alike. While it began with T-shirts, the word was soon on billboards, political posters, baseball caps, and much more. It permeated every aspect of human life. Even teenagers who dwell in the world of acronyms and emojis signed off their texts with "Kitjovistinope" – the largest word in their vocabularies. The first colony on the red planet is said to include a Kitjovistinope district – the cultural hub of the new frontier.

Everyday activities were described using this word. The lack of a clear definition adding to its versatility. It even invaded the stage with an avant-garde version of Hamlet quoting: *To Kitjovistinope or not to Kitjovistinope, that is the question: Whether 'tis nobler in the mind to suffer the slings and arrows of outrageous fortune, or to take up a brush and by Kitjovistinope, end them.*

"It means so much more than just plain old '*Be*', you know," wrote James T. Worthingtonhamshire of *Snub Magazine*'s literary column. "The sense of not knowing what it means…that's the magic. The inventor of this word is the hero of our generation! Whoever he or she may be."

The world of graphic design was most heavily impacted by the word. Its creation was compared to when Stanley Morison designed the *Times New Roman* font for the *Times of London* in 1932. "That shifted the way we consumed journalism and read print," said Ms. Patent the Bright Report's calligrapher. "Kitjovistinope did the same for slogans, only so much more."

But the praise was all but universal. The literary world – or at least, the reading world – have not been as welcoming to Kitjovistinope as other sectors. Our own Jacques Bord of the Bright Report's literary desk was less enthusiastic, commenting: "the fact that we put so much stock in gibberish and jargon is what got us in this mess in the first place – look at the state of the world – a nonsense word won't change it or even save the publishing world."

This journalist had to know the definition of the word – despite dissenting voices from the rest of the art world.

"The point of it – the magic of it – is that it can't be defined," wrote Mr Truedeck of the *Timely Journal* – the Bright Report's rival publication. "The art of it is its mystery – to define it is to bring Kitjovistinope down to the level of language."

This is a perfectly romantic sentiment, indeed. But this journalist – who has spent the last few months receiving cryptic texts from her teenage son containing only this word – had to get to the bottom of this.

And so, I came to Forty-Seven Ramshackle Lane. The place was neat – as described above – but there were subtle changes. The 'Studio' had been transformed into a printing room. Each room – overcrowded with carefully arranged tat – had hints of the word's encroachment on their lives. There were framed pictures with it written in different fonts – gone were *Austere Landscapes numbers one through thirteen*.

The pile of letters from Mrs Bradshaw of number Forty-Nine Ramshackle Lane had dwindled. "We just reply with Kitjovistinope," said Mr Krinkle laughing throatily. "That shuts her up."

Indeed, there was an air of jovial satisfaction about the couple. "We're happier," he told me. This was confirmed by enthusiastic nods from Mrs Krinkle. "I can be messy with the colors and she makes sure that I'm neat with the letters. It's something we bring into the world together."

I was given the tour and a free selection of T-shirts and promotional stickers.

"Who needs to measure candles," said Mrs Krinkle. We

eventually settled in the lounge for tea. She was knitting a pair of baby booties with Kitjovistinope crocheted across them. "It's much more fulfilling making sure that Worbal's letters are all properly spaced."

She had, in fact, given up her job at *Vonnegut's Candle and Lamp Manufacturing Co.* Even after being offered a job as chairwoman. "They wanted to put it on scented candles, you see. We let them – for a price, but I did not have it in me to keep measuring things that…do not last. This," she held up her knitting at this point, "this fills a hole, you know?"

After hearing their accounts of 'the day it happened', I began probing the couple on the issue of definitions. They were reluctant to lift the curtain, to say the least.

"It means everything," Mr Krinkle insisted. "Everything you want it to mean and so much more. It means not giving up when all you've known is failure. It also means failure in a good way. It also means none of that. That's the magic of it, you see?"

This journalist was not moved. I thanked them sincerely for the tea, the tour, and the T-shirts. Hopefully, my teenager would be roused to articulation by a few stickers from the artists themselves.

Mr Krinkle had a fresh printing run of Kitjovistinope doggie outfits to attend to. There was an odd melancholy to his toils: a man deep in the autumn of his life, printing his word on anything and everything, only to be obscured by it. Everyone knew Kitjovistinope – no one knew his name.

The business of letting me out fell to the woman of the house. Mrs Krinkle by herself was the inquisitive sort. She enquired after my son. She wanted to know his age (to the exact hour), his height, weight, and eye color.

"Blue like his dad's," I told her. "The rest of him is me if you know what I mean. Just wish he'd talk to me for a day in his life."

"He will come round, I'm sure," she said. "You have him, and that matters a lot."

It was then that Mrs Krinkle told me not only the definition of Kitjovistinope but also what it meant. The former was surprising – disappointing even. The latter was something this journalist suspected ever since she sat down to tea.

I bid her goodbye, leaving her to a life of measuring – a life of avoiding the loneliness of even numbers. I phoned my son on the way home – it went to voicemail, as usual, but I spoke my mind, even though I knew it was Kitjovistinope. I told him what he meant to me in both the rational world of measurements and the irrational world of sentiment and the art of being. Eventually, he will listen to it and I will deserve the roll of his bright eyes.

With my heart full of purpose, I sat down at my typewriter and wrote this account. I could tell you the true meaning of the word, dear valued reader of the Bright Report, but I am not going to.

Unsolved mysteries are annoying – like unscratched mosquito bites, but much like this simile, nothing good can come of scratching this mystery. Alright, that is a jumbled metaphor, but suffice to say that Kitjovistinope is what it is.

However, I will attempt to define it for myself. You may take it or leave it – as they say.

Kitjovistinope: *noun*. A sincere, yet ultimately foolish endeavor that comes at the cost of everything else.

AND/OR

Kitjovistinope: *verb*. To struggle and persevere even if the outcome is certain failure.

LITERATURE: THE CHIPROCK RECLUSE
BY JAQUES BORD

Note to Mr Lazen F. Balding Jr. III, Editor-in-Chief of the Bright Report:

<u>Do not</u> *publish this story. It is what you commissioned and contains the truth – a truth that will ruin me. And do not presume to think that you can get away with publishing this in one of those "Best of" collections you are planning. Not only will I deny every detail of the story, but you will also have my resignation letter on your desk in the morning.*

The storm was horrible. I should describe it better – illustrate the tempest we found ourselves in with all my literary prowess. I could mention the rocking of the boat, the thunderous thunder, the blinding lightning, and the shouting of the men running across the deck. Perhaps I can cast away the clichés and attempt something original: my eggs benedict was making its presence known in the back of my throat, my mind was treading water, and my guts were gurgling.

No.

"*The storm was horrible*" sums it up.

I, Jacques Bord, literary critic extraordinaire and senior writer for the Bright Report, hate islands as much as I hate clichés.

Water on all sides. No escape from the locals.

But here I am – making the crossing to Chiprock Island in a tub clinking with empty whiskey bottles. Oh, Mr Balding, in his infinite wisdom has thought it good and sound to send me to this little slice of nowhere. He sent me here to sniff out a cliché of all things: a reclusive writer.

*

How did I get here, you ask? What did I do to deserve this?

I would like to believe that the Bright Report is chasing trends. There I said it. Edit it out – I dare you. As I am the only bibliophilic hack the Report has, I was sent to track down a sensational new voice in the world of…*genre*…fiction. This certainly was not some kind of cold revenge for my (less than) favorable review of our editor's niece's (so called) modern takes on the Brontë works. Certainly not. The man agreed with me at the time that…

Well, I digress.

Before I was subjected to this saltwater hell referred to locally as "*a little paddle across the pond*", the world was taken by storm by a modest collection of short stories. A saccharin anthology of slice-of-life meets H.P. Lovecraft fishmen. Light-hearted fantasy, some might call it – not my usual grazing grounds as a critic, as regular readers well know.

But say one thing for Jacques Bord, say that he has an open mind. Open enough.

I enjoyed the eight stories of *The Aquatic Acquaintance* well enough. The author, one Shamiana Fim, achieved an unlikely sense of believability in his/her merging of the mundane and the unreal. He or she convinced enough readers of this brilliance to achieve bestseller status in several countries.

The world was hungry to know who Shamiana Fim was. Perhaps it was a pen name or the initials of several authors – something tedious like that. There were no clues. Even the publishers of the collection were at a loss.

You have a go:

S H A M I A N A F I M

I got stuck on the first four letters and stopped bothering with it.

Adding to the mystery is the fact that there is no author bio and no real geographic information other than the quaint island setting described in each of the stories. There was the occasional mention of Svalbard, Kyrgyzstan, and the Hebridean island of Staffa, but nothing concrete on the setting itself. Ms. Pheme from the Linguistics desk assured us that she detected a slight Rhode Island accent to the dialogue – something which she insists the author is trying to cover up. If they had asked me – and they did not – the characters' accents read like cartoon pirates.

Nevertheless, my mind was at ease. We would never track this Fim person down. Mr Balding would never send me on such an assignment. I could stick to real literature – the prose that really said something.

That would have been easy. But – as you know – things are never easy for the protagonist.

Enter my colleague, Mr Carmichael Carmichael, travel journalist extraordinaire. He is the kind of man who drinks tea with his pinky finger at an exact angle one moment and then spear-fishes with the tribes of Papua New Guinea the next. The sort of man who knows the names of all the Himalayan peaks – not just the tallest one, and not just what arrogant Europeans call them, either. The sort of man who travels everywhere. He only needed a few paragraphs to solve the mystery.

"That's old Chiprock, dear boy," he told me. "Capital place. It has a real…how do I put it…story-book appeal. Try the trout special!"

The man was quite impressed with this achievement. I really must thank him once I extract myself from the jaws of Poseidon. But the time for creative retribution would come later.

That brings us back to my ordeal by boat.

*

The storm raged on.

I asked our captain – a grizzled man lost in the woods of his mid-fifties whose wobbly gait I should have seen as a measure of his sobriety – why could we not wait for the weather to clear? He assured me that he had 'seen worse'.

I gazed into the jagged black water that surrounded (and occasionally spilled into) our little tug. The milky eye of a pale cetacean peering at us from the surf was the only thing that seemed as if it could match the description of 'worse'.

But on we went. The crew shouted. The wind howled. My eggs benedict made a break for it. I ruined my best jacket that day.

All for some recluse.

Alas, Neptune did not take me into his embrace. Half-drowned and carrying a pint of ocean in my Oxfords, we emerged on the shore of Chiprock Island. The dock – if you could call the rotten plank collection that – did little to display the island's virtues. There were only rocky cliffs and rocky shores. A muddy track was the only path into the village.

Several disillusioned crew members and I flopped ourselves onto the moldy pier like the day's catch. Insults flew. I bid them thanks in my own special way, but they did not seem to appreciate my outstretched finger.

"Look at the boat," Mr Foreshone – the commander of our doomed dingy – ordered with an accusatory tone. "It ain't gonna fix itself."

"How long?" I ventured. I could not see the opposite shore anymore – just purple darkness.

The wind whipped around the man, his white beard flapping. He looked as mad as Ahab. "Aye, should be re'dy in a day or so – tha' be if the lads work 'ard and the wee drizzle clears."

I originally intended to spend no more than a few hours on Chiprock – for one, I did not bring any luggage. I was tempted to repeat my hand gesture.

Fortunately, a fight broke out amongst the deck hands regarding wages and/or the virtues of someone's mother and/or girlfriend.

I left them to their colloquial dealings and limped my way into town. The storm calmed a little as I ascended the muddy track. Patches of sky were mockingly clear.

Soon the muddy trail became a cobbled main road. Crooked stone buildings emerged from the fog. Rural folk appeared.

Perhaps it was the beret that made them stare – certainly, there was no one dressed as I was in sight. More likely was the fact that I was leaking like a holy bucket. I ignored their looks of suspicion and surprise and tried to light a cigarette. My matches were damp – everything was waterlogged.

If only we set off a few minutes later – I would have been spared the indignation. I would have had my customary broody smoke upon arrival. That was usually the best first impression to make – not this dripping mess.

I found a spot beneath a roof overhang. The bulky metal structure looked like a warehouse of some kind. It smelt of fish and was decorated with a network of rust.

A stranger held out a lighter. The warmth of its little flame nourished the soul. Said stranger had appeared with the suddenness of lightning. She was a woman – maybe in her late fifties. Her hair – strands of grey and dull blonde – was ratcheted back in a tight ponytail. The skin of her face was sun-wrinkled, and her hands were rough.

She wordlessly lit her own cigarette.

A quiet moment of dripping followed.

"You swim here?" she asked without looking.

"Close enough," I replied.

We stood beneath the overhang and watched the lightning stutter in the distance.

"You the reporter," she said. It did not feel like a question.

I nodded as I wrung out my beret. There was a bath-worth of water in it. I was also becoming increasingly aware that my notebook and Dictaphone were weighing down my inside jacket pocket.

"Supposed to be," I said.

"You'll be wanting to stay at the Paddle and Orr, then," she said. She took a deep drag of her cigarette and expelled it with a long sigh. She watched the drops from the roof edge dive through the smoke cloud. She looked at me for the first time. Her grey eyes shone with the light of the storm. "Don't have the trout special," she said amid a chorus of thunder.

I assured her that I would not. She took advantage of the pause in the deluge and stomped off towards the docks. Any attempt to ascertain her identity or her business was flatly ignored.

Once I finished my cigarette, I squelched my way up Chiprock's main street. Most of the village's quaint little houses were built along its relentless incline. The cobbles glittered – much like they did in the author's stories.

As I progressed, there was the occasional squeal of a rusty window being opened or the laughter of children running to post-storm freedom. Every inhabitant – including the jubilant youths – regarded my waterlogged state with quiet amusement. My soggy hellos went unanswered.

Then I found it.

Moss covered stone made up the structure of the Paddle and Orr. Dark green window frames gave a view of a dark interior – like the hovel of some fairy tale hermit.

The oily patrons fell silent as I stepped in. The sound of dripping accompanied each squelching footstep. I beached myself upon a corner seat and felt the weight of my fatigue. A great thirst was within my salty bones as the tide of sea water receded from me.

"Sherry," I wheezed at the serving girl. To describe the look she gave me as "funny" would not entirely do it justice.

The patrons soon tired of my strangeness and went about their mundane chitter-chatter. They were certainly strange to me, now that I came to think of it. They were hunched and dirty. The exact nature of the dirt was hard to define – each patron seemed to be worn down somehow. Like the barnacled belly of an old trawler.

I hate islands. I distrust island people. A cruel thought struck me: this could be a leper colony.

A grubby bookshelf lent against the wall next to the fireplace. It was packed with waterlogged magazines and chubby dictionaries. To my surprise, several pristine copies of *The Aquatic Acquaintance* were in attendance.

Damn my luck: this is the right place.

The waitress placed the glass of ambrosia down and gave me a searching look. She too seemed as tide worn as a costal cliff: all crows' nests and jagged edges. Her eyes like dull pearls settled on my shoes. Evidently, a puddle was forming.

"BETTER TAKE 'EM OFF," she foghorned. "TOES WILL GET DER ROT, THEN YOU GOT LOADS O' TROUBLE!"

Lepers stared – I could feel them. I thanked her softly, hoping to lower her volume.

"WE 'AVE SOME SOCKS," she said. Her voice bounced off the walls. Her voice was giving me tinnitus.

"Umm…thank you," I managed. "And…perhaps, if not too inconvenient…a roo-…a clean room."

"RIGHT YER ARE," she boomed. "THAT'LL BE THE ROYAL SUITE, ONLY ONE WE'S GOT GOING!"

I cringed. Even people in the street were privy to the conversation. "Yes, thank you," I said. I hoped that I could lead by example by speaking softly. "I would like to book it."

"HOW LONG WILL THAT BE DEN? HERE FOR BUSINESS OR PLEASURE?"

I assured her that I would only be for a night and that it certainly was not for pleasure. The establishment was silent – as if every drinker had been listening.

I stopped the waitress from wondering off. "Perhaps you can help me," I said leaning in close.

"SPEAK UP LOVE!"

My low voice persisted. "I am looking for Shamiana Fim. Do you know where I can find him or her?"

"SHAMIANA FIM, YER SAY?" she said most audibly.

Several wooden chairs creaked. A number of beer mugs were put down.

"Yes," I said pointing to the bookcase. "The author of that book - Shamiana Fim. Does this person live on the island somewhere? Have you met them?"

The waitress scratched her chin and chewed her lip. "CAN'T SAY I 'AVE, LOVE. WHAT DID YOU SAY YOUR BUSINESS WAS AGAIN?"

"I didn't say," I said. The atmosphere was thick and threatening, as if I announced my undying support for a rival football club. "I must have the wrong place then," I ventured. "I'll be off in the morning. Umm…with the tide, as they say."

The woman seemed satisfied by this and left me to my sherry. Conversation returned to the Paddle and Orr like a phantom wave.

I began removing my shoes wondering if the "rot" she was referring too was the big "L". A local sidled up to me in my distraction. I nearly threw a soggy boot at the poor man out of fright.

"Here about 'em fish stories den?" he asked. He was covered in grey stubble and sported a fine pipe. Without an invitation, the lump of a man pulled up a chair and tamped down his tobacco.

I nodded.

The old man smiled. "Der all true, ye know," he said smiling with teeth so jagged they all seemed to vie for the best spot in his mouth. "Ev'ry word. I seen 'em meself – God's truth. Best thing to 'appen ta Chiprock in all me years. Saves on the fishin', ye know? All 'em presents they brung us."

The silence had returned – everyone was listening. I glanced about and met their grinning stares. I understood: the old man was not senile. He was testing the outsider's gullibility.

I told him that he was the undiscovered comedic superstar of his generation and went about my business of removing my soggy socks. The other drinkers laughed.

"Beware the storm tonight, lad," said the old man solemnly. He returned to his original table. He was the only one with a stern expression.

I fumed silently and resolved to put some food in my stomach. Remembering my smoking acquaintance's warning, I steered clear of the trout special. Good old fish and chips did wonders.

While I leave cuisine critique to my colleague Ms. Dumont, I will say that the Paddle and Orr fish and chips revives the half-drowned. The dish came with a complimentary red ribbon which was explained as being 'traditional'.

Thereafter I retired to my room and – oh, dear loyal reader – was I in for a night.

*

The storm was horrible. Luckily, this time I was indoors and on a bed. The springs groaned as I pulled my blankets about my head. The terror of thunder still had a hold over me. Rain splashed the narrow windows. I blessed the threadbare blankets and the borrowed socks.

The occasional illumination of the room cast strange shadows on the grubby walls. It was gloomy – yes that is the word. Gloomy with the sparkle of electricity, as if something were about to happen. If I were some Hollywood bombshell in the shower, I would fear for my life. I tried to recall the faces in the tap room earlier – no, none of them looked like Mr Hitchcock. Besides, you would not find me in a shower any time soon – I have seen enough water for a lifetime.

It was when I shifted my glass of water away from me on the bedside table that I heard it. Not the roll of thunder or the howl of the wind – no, no clichés at all. It was a *slap-slap, squelch-squelch* sound coming down the hallway.

It made my heart stop. I must have imagined it. No. There it is again. It is getting closer. It is coming here – to my room.

Lightning flashed; thunder rattled the windows.

Regular readers of my column know that I often take issue with gormless horror movie teens who – against all forms of sense, common or otherwise – abandon relative safety to inspect the source of some disturbance or ungodly sound. Well, those of you who write in to complain about my complaining will be happy to know that I let myself down.

Like a gormless horror movie teen, I rose from my bed and approached the door. The more soft-hearted readers among you might be comforted by the fact that I kept my blanket at the ready, should the need for self-defense arise.

The sound grew louder. *Slap-slap, squelch-squelch.*

I cracked the door open a half an inch. I took care to keep the handle down to prevent it from squealing. It took me several seconds to find the courage to peek.

There was something in the hallway. A dark figure outlined in the occasional flash from the window behind it. It seemed to be limping towards me – dripping as it went. This instantly roused my sympathies: this must be another poor soul who had made use of Mr Foreshone's ferry service.

The half-drowned sod moaned as he walked.

I was resolved to cast off my blanket and rush to his side with a warm handshake. Let the poor chap know that he is among civilized folk despite the bleak evidence to the contrary.

Lightning flashed again.

One of the man's eyes caught the light.

I slammed the door shut, leant against it, and tried to catch my breath. Now, this is where things get hard to explain. I am sure of what I saw, but I am also sure that it was impossible.

I was tired and I was probably coming down with some form of pneumonia (or leprosy, jury still out), and there was all that talk of fishmen and rural folklore. It could only have been a hallucination.

I made sure that the door was properly closed (there was no key), and I returned to bed with the blankets covering even my face – I was a sick man, you see. I told myself that I needed sleep – all would be better in the morning.

That was when the hallucination knocked on the door.

Gathering my courage, I told it to go away.

There was another knock. The hallucination spoke. It was not a human voice – not exactly. It clicked and bubbled through a throat that was not accustomed to air.

"Mon…monsieur…Bee…Bord," it gurgled. "I am here…to…"

Lightning flashed. The roll of thunder almost drowned out the squeak of the door handle.

My shattered mind had a lucid thought: *run*. Grabbing my blanket and the soggy remains of my jacket, I pushed past the slimy figure just as it entered. Webbed fingers clawed at me. I screamed, but I never looked back. That would have made it too real.

The creature burbled at me as I ran down the hall. "Across…da…pond…Monsieur…I…ta-take you…"

I arrived in the tap room more by falling down the stairs than descending them. Luckily, there was no one around to be subjected to my foul language. The boards creaked above – the creature was in pursuit.

Evidently, I had forgotten my pants and my notebook. Without the latter, a journalist was practically naked. The chill-damp jacket would have to do. I escaped into the night and onto the rainy streets of Chiprock. It seemed like a sane plan at the time, dear reader, but surely the fever had taken me. I ran across the cobbled streets in my boxers. Soggy socks splashed through puddles.

I headed down main street and towards the pier. The occasional flash lit the slippery way. In my blind panic, I did not notice them at first. The streets were busy. Hunched figures were proceeding up and down the thoroughfare. Each flash glinted off flat eyes the size of dinner plates. Gaping mouths. Silvery scales.

These creatures went about their business, untroubled by the literary critic having a mental breakdown. Some opened garden gates with webbed fingers and walked up to front doors. Others bore buckets of fish. I could have sworn – in my fever haze – that a few of the buckets had bright red ribbons on them.

This was a nightmare. At that moment I was fatefully sure of that. This is what happens when you are half-drowned, and you have subjected your subconscious to genre fiction.

I kept running. I needed to get off this damned island.

Through the rain I found the warehouse that I had my arrival smoke at. The door was ajar, spilling warm orange light into the street.

Sanctuary.

I rushed in and startled the occupants. Here amid the boxes and containers were two figures: the first was my smoking companion – the woman with the severe ponytail, the second was…well…it is hard to explain. I was certain – at the time – that it was a man with a misshapen head: fish-like, absurdly large eyes, gills, a gaping mouth. A cigarette was dangling from the latter. Perhaps strangest of all was the fact that the creature was wearing a flat cap, dungarees, and rubber boots.

The world became a blur. I remember hitting the muddy floor of the warehouse.

The next thing I remembered was a splitting headache. I sat bolt upright. I was in a lumpy bed, covered by a coarse blanket. Candlelight flickered. I seemed to be in some cozy attic room – judging by the corrugated ceiling. The rain was softly drumming on it. The walls were shelves – shelves stuffed with dogeared volumes.

The critic within arose. He scoffed at the rank of books closest to him: pulp nonsense, romance, science fiction, ten-penny thrillers. But as my eye travelled along the shelves, I encountered classics – the greats of English, French, Russian, and even American writers. The masters of their craft. As I followed the shelves around the room, I was delighted to find rare books: a first edition *Tamerlane* (signed by Poe, no less), a Greek work which details the plot of *Margites*, a copy of the *Silent Symphony* (author listed as 'You and Me'), and two lost Shakespeare works (*Love's Labor Won* and *Cardenio*).

They may have been forgeries (or lingering hallucinations), but I was certainly intrigued. Who owned such a magnificent collection? What literary loner lived here?

This must be the bolt hole of the enigmatic Shamiana Fim.

Reluctantly averting my gaze from the shelves, I scanned the rest of the room for clues. There was the lumpy bed – yes – a double. There was a fish tank bubbling away in the corner – light, filter, and whatever makes the bubbles, but no fish.

Fish – dear Lord.

Focus.

A table with a lamp – a reading nook. An ashtray rested on an old magazine. On closer inspection an old copy of the Bright Report with a bookmark at one of my old reviews – an intriguing find. It took a moment to realize my ignorance: the ashtray. It was full of the same brand that my smoking acquaintance enjoyed upon arrival.

Just as I believed the mystery solved, a metal stairwell leading up to the attic began clanging. Someone was coming.

"Ah, madam," I said. "Thank you for coming to my rescue. I believe that I was overcome by…by…"

Language left me once the figure reached the top of the stairs. It carried a tray of eggs and bacon. A cup of coffee steamed. The figure placed it on the reading table.

"Mon…monsieur…Bah…Bord," it burbled. "For … yer … health. Good … eat … en. Would … you … like … dah … mornin … paper?"

I backed into the corner of the room. My eyes were deceiving me. A half-man, half-fish was standing in front of me – wearing a gown.

Remembering my manners, I blurted out a thank you.

Webbed hands gestured for me to sit down. I obeyed stiffly and cautiously.

The creature's massive fisheyes watched me as I took up my knife and fork.

"Ho ... hope ... you ... like ... em ... sunny ... si ... side ... up." It pronounced the final word with a kind of guttural pop.

I began eating with the unfeeling passion of a man soon to face the firing squad. Was it going to eat me? Drag me into the watery depths? Worst of all, I feared for my reputation should I ever commit this story to paper.

As I settled into my meal, I found that I also settled in his company. Before I knew it, I was interviewing the creature. I learnt that he – for he was thus – wrote under the name Shamiana Fim – nothing more than a clever anagram. His true name was unpronounceable to the human tongue and defied phonetic commitment to the page.

My smoking acquaintance was Caroline, his wife of eleven years. I did not enquire after the mechanics of such a relationship, but I was made to understand that it was passionate and loving.

His story was not unique. In fact, nearly every resident of Chiprock had a fish-person friend or relative. It was accepted and welcome. They paid the residence in fresh fish in exchange for sanctuary during horrible storms. Apparently, the world beneath the waves was unsafe during such weather – not only because of strong currents, but also because ancient gods woke to wreak havoc under the waves.

The latter point made me worry and I decided not to pursue that line of questioning.

This particular fishman had a lucky escape on one stormy night. Caroline offered him a smoke and a place to recover. In his convalescence, she introduced him to the world of fiction. He fell in love with stories and the woman who read them to him. Now, after a decade of marriage and possessed of a fully grown library, he decided to try his hand as an author.

"I ... row ... wrote ... what ... made ... it ... mag ... magical ... for ... me ... an ... and ... Caroline ... Its...our...life..."

The pieces were beginning to fit. The stories were not strange Lovecraftian slice-of-life mashups, they told the story of a real couple and their hometown.

I finished my breakfast and nursed my coffee. There was a red ribbon tied to the handle of the mug. My aquatic friend explained that a sunken container – just off the harbor – was full of haberdashery supplies.

My ex-wife called me many things, but 'sentimental' was not one of them. I am still not entirely sure why I pocketed the ribbon.

"I can't write this interview," I told him solemnly. "No one would ever believe me. They'll think I'm crazy."

The fishman nodded. He told me to write it anyway – to write it for myself. "You … have … seen … mah … much. All that … you … you … see … changes … you. Especially … if … if … you … can … eat … break … fast … with … someone … tha … that … frightens … you. We … just … need … a … a … story … or … tah … two … to … know … that … we … we … are … all … human."

He thanked me for my company and left me to my thoughts. I sat in silence for a while. I scanned through some of the books. Smoked a cigarette. I paged through the old Bright Report and read my old review. It is one of those where I savaged a debut author for mixing fantasy fiction with 'serious' literature. Those were enjoyable to write – indeed, they were apparently my most read work. But something was not right.

I dressed and gathered my things. There was a fresh (and dry) notebook in my jacket pocket. I gave one final look at the book collection before clanging down the metal stairs.

The storm had cleared by the time I left the warehouse. The weather was beautiful, in fact. Townsfolk went about their lives. Children played in the street. Red ribbons hung from garden gates and bicycle handles – small reminders of their kindness. The cobbles – washed clean by the storm – shone in the sunlight.

I greeted the passers-by. They greeted back. The air was fresh. The grubby buildings appeared less so. I had judged the place as another backwater – a place where life was slow and dull. But on this fine morning it seemed like something more – a sanctuary away from the cruel and stormy world.

I fingered the ribbon in my pocket as I walked down to the docks.

"Good morning, Captain," I said.

He and his men were hammering a fresh log into place. At least the port side of the vessel was watertight now.

"Aye," said the Captain. He seemed less red in the face than he did the day before. "Won't be ready till tomorrow, sorry."

"That's fine," I said. "There's no rush."

I strolled along the shore, found a nice big rock, and opened my brand-new notebook. The pages were crisp, and they had that new-anything-can-happen smell to them.

I wrote.

Have breakfast with the one you fear. Tell a story. Listen to a story. And remember that, at the end, we are all human — give or take a fin or two.

SPORT: THE DERBY
BY CHARLINE RATANANG

We rounded the bend. We were almost going fast enough to blow off my racing turban. But that could have been the stiff breeze. Farlingworth was still going strong. My saddle was still rigidly attached to his shell as I pulled on his eyestalks to keep us on course.

We were about to face the true test of skill and adhesion: the vertical ascent. Make it through this stint unscathed (and attached) and Farlingworth and I were in good stead. Not many riders – nay, not many journalists – could claim to finish a stage of the Monstrous Patagonian Snail Derby in one piece.

I aimed to change this.

My snail – valiant Farlingworth – was a prime specimen of *Achatina giganticus*, the pride of the Tanzanian racing stables. He[1] moved with a smooth grace, covering nearly 60cm per minute. While there is little proof of this, I hoped that the racing stripes and flames I painted on the shell the night before added a few millimeters per capillary action (or MPCA as the initiated refer to it). This was not a bad speed. In fact, it was almost "up there with the pros" – as they say.

There were several competitors snailing their way up the massive

---

[1] Technically, Farlingworth – along with the other snails – are "dioecious". The trainer assured me that meant that it was either a he or a she – not quite the same as being both at the same time. Be that as it may, Farlingworth looked like a "he" to me.

cliff face. The leaders were not even a third of the way up, meaning that I was not as far behind as I had feared. There was no sign of Mr Atkins from The Timely Journal[2] on his borrowed thoroughbred, *Clink*.

These two facts spurred me on. Even Farlingworth whose sleepy eyes stared off into the middle distance seemed slightly more energized.

The dangers of the sport became clear once we approached the rock face: no more than a few yards from where my snail and I would make our sticky climb, was a scene. A yellow flag blew in the wind. Marshals surrounded a fallen competitor. Bits of shell littered the ground.

This is never something a journalist wants to see – especially when she is about to attempt something so dangerous. I swallowed hard, steadied my nerve as best as I could, and pushed the snail's eyestalks forward.

I later learned that the casualty was Monsieur Chevrolet riding *Malchance III*. The Frenchman was lucky to escape with minor bruises and a sprained wrist. The snail, I am sad to report, lived up to his name.

Farlingworth sailed up to the wall. His instinct was to turn away – to avoid the sheer face entirely. It took some coaxing in the form of soft words and whistling his favorite song[3] before he took to the barrier. Gravity shifted as we began our climb.

This is it.

One hand clung onto his eyestalk – a gentle grip, anything more would be disastrous. The other hand was white knuckled on the saddle. The harness cut into me in uncomfortable places. I hoped the nylon straps would hold.

In the old days, of course, there were no such luxuries as reinforced turbans and seatbelts. Only grit, determination, and muscular thighs. The latter is the source of the bowlegged snail rider stereotype modern competitors detest.

I blessed modern advancements in safety as Farlingworth climbed. The ground steadily receded behind us. I tried not to look down – or back. The entire experience was highly disorienting.

Several competitors ahead of me were veering left or right – their

---

[2] The Bright Report's rival publication.

[3] *Seven Nation Army* by the White Stripes – not the easiest thing to whistle, I know.

weight proved too much for the snails. Despite every effort by the riders, the slimy steeds were arching back down to ground level. It was a true test of discipline and strength.

Farlingworth kept climbing at a steady pace. The shift in gravity hardly bothered him.

I came up on another competitor: Justin Martin of Canada riding *Captain Crunch*. The snail had retracted into its shell. The rider was tapping on it, shouting threats of encouragement, and the occasional swear word. This was not an unusual situation for the Canadian as reliability issues had plagued him all season.

We sailed on sheepishly, trying not to be a target for his frustration.

A racing turban tumbled. I caught it out of instinct – nearly losing my seating. I glanced up.

Two snails side-by-side. Two riders clinging onto each other. One was three-time derby winner, Clara Van Hereson of the Netherlands riding *Clyde van Dusen*. The other was the New Zealander, Hickson Wisson, on *Waikikamukau* – also a previous winner of the event.

The snails were trying to cross one another's paths. Neither one relented, resulting in a slow roadblock. I mistook the rider's embrace for a wrestling match – each trying to make the other's ride give way. But as we approached, I realized that Wisson was trying to resecure Van Hereson's harness. The two shells rubbing together must have snapped something. She clung onto Wisson with all her might – her fingers bunching up his collar. Her ginger hair whipping in the wind.

There was no reason for the New Zealander to help the woman. They had often been bitter rivals – one barely edging out the other at each meeting of the snails. They were such fierce competitors that one refused to even enter a race if the other was not in the running. I admired their passion. Now I marveled at the sportsmanship.

I shouted up at them. I had to help if I could.

"You're going to ruin your own race," said a voice slightly below me. I glanced down to see the smug face of Toshi Atkins. He had caught up to me. His steed, Clink, a slightly redder specimen of snail-kind, eyed Farlingworth menacingly.

"But they could fall," I said. I spurred my snail onwards. At the back of my mind, I worried that an increase of speed might compromise his suction.

"They know the risks," said Atkins. He spurred his snail on too, trying to draw level with me. The man always made my blood boil.

We neared the stricken riders. Wisson had managed to fashion a new harness from one of his own stirrups. Both of their snails had retracted into their shells by now.

"You alright there?" I called as Farlingworth lazily navigated around the pair.

"Close call," said the New Zealander.

"Oh, Hickson," said Clara. Her grip on Wisson had morphed into a tight hug. "If you weren't here…I…I."

"You're fine," said Wisson as he bashfully pulled himself free. "Anyone would have done the same." The man glanced at me, red faced. "She was having trouble," he said.

"Good man," I said. I threw Clara's racing turban back to her. That is when I caught sight of Atkins and Clink crawling up the far side of the couple. The brigand was taking the lead.

Wisson and Van Hereson followed my gaze. They knew that Atkins and I were rivals.

"Go get him," said Clara. "We will take a while to get our dears out of their shells." Her and Hickson's eyes locked. "We're not in a rush."

A simple fact dawned on me. The fierce competitors had passion, indeed. Just not the kind that I had suspected.

I moved Farlingworth's stalks forward. We continued our climb, sights set firmly on Clink and his rider. The journalist smiled back at me.

"Told you!" he said. "Stop to help and you'll ruin your race. You'll never catch me now."

I was falling behind by a few centimeters every second. That red devil of his sure could move. Atkins was an accomplished sportsman in his own right, of course, but the man was muscular and bulky. His weight would have been a disadvantage if he were riding an ordinary monstrous snail. But Clink was anything but ordinary. Not only had it come from a long line of thoroughbred racing champions, but it was also fed on an exclusive diet of Saint Sebaldus olives and over-sugared ground cereal. This resulted in an animal with great bursts of speed and a low longevity. Not that the latter bothered the breeders much, as Sebaldine Escargot sold at a premium.

"Come on, Farlingworth," I said. Those flames had to be good for something. He bubbled, seemingly in reply. That is as close as a racing snail came to frothing at the mouth.

Every unusual sport I undertook – every single one of them – Atkins was there. The man delighted in trouncing me in each endeavor. I must admit that I took pleasure in doing the same to him. However, taking advantage of the misfortune of other competitors like this… Well, I had to draw the line somewhere.

I was so focused on catching Clink that I hardly noticed that we were almost at the top of the cliff. Wind tugged at my overalls. It howled along the sheer rock wall. The sky was bruising into a deep purple blue as the sun set somewhere on the other side of the mountain. The derby was almost over and there were two snails far in the lead. Snails ridden by sportswriters, no less.

"I'm almost there," said Atkins. "Come on, Ratanang! Is that all you've got?"

One must keep one's composure at times like these. I bit my tongue. One could not waste time or concentration on banter. I felt Farlingworth narrow his eyes at the man. He bubbled again. His shell shook with the effort of keeping up.

"Come on," said Atkins. "Want me to sprinkle some salt on you? Could be a good motivator." He laughed manically.

"Focus, Farlingworth," I whispered. There was a great lurch from the snail. I felt a strange weightlessness in the pit of my stomach. We were slipping. The world went into rewind as the top edge of the cliff was steadily becoming further and further away. Farlingworth was slowly sliding down, leaving a wet track of stickiness. I tried not to panic – tried not to look back at the void below us.

I had two options: (1) spur the poor thing on and risk falling, or (2) give up the chase and regain some suction. I grimaced at the silhouette of Clink and his infuriating rider. There was only one right choice in the moment.

I squeezed Farlingworth's eyestalk firmly. He reacted by retracting into his shell. I clung on as he settled and exhaled a long sigh. At least we stopped slipping. I folded in on myself and rested on my arms ignoring the howl of the wind. Exhaustion was setting in – that and the bitter taste of losing to The Timely Journal's finest.

"I thought I'd never see the day," said a voice.

I looked up. Atkins had turned Clink around and was now in spitting distance.

"I've never seen you give up," he said. I had never seen him without his smug smile, so I guess we were even.

"Who says I gave up?" I asked. "I'm saving the snail."

The red snail bubbled menacingly. Farlingworth bubbled in reply from the safety of his shell. His shell lurched as he cautiously re-emerged. I carefully grasped his eyestalks.

"Come on, Charline," said Atkins. "It's no fun without an equal challenge."

"Was that a compliment?"

He smiled his stupid smug smile. "You're assuming that I'm talking about you."

I told him to shut his mouth as I spurred Farlingworth on. It would take him a while to turn Clink around. He had the straight-line speed, certainly, but he could not turn on a doormat.

This advantage was short-lived: we were neck-and-neck as we crawled over the lip of the cliff. The light of the sunset dazzled us as the world righted itself. A crowd cheered. Spectators from all over the world were lined up on either side of the final stretch. There it was: the finish line, a shiny piece of ribbon decorated with countless sponsors.

Atkins and I exchanged glances. Our snails were spurred on. They bubbled angrily at each other. To us it felt like a high-octane chase to the end. To the audience – who had run out of cheering breath – it seemed slightly less so. Some even had time to fetch a hotdog and come back.

Farlingworth, of course, stood little chance in a straight line. We watched in dismay as the red snail and the smug journalist cut through the ribbon. The crowd – happy to finally see some action – burst into roaring applause. I would have applauded too – after all, it was not every derby that you had a first-time winner. But exhaustion had taken hold. All I cared about at that moment was getting out of the harness and having a well-deserved lie down.

There were cheers, champagne, and victory laurels for the riders, and celebratory celery for the snails. The top three were presented with medals and a cheque from Invocorp – the race's main sponsor. The latter was presented by a bespectacled man in a lab coat. It was an all-round good time.

I avoided talking to Mr Atkins – I had had enough of his smugness for the moment. There was always next time – not that I was keeping score or anything. The riders celebrated deep into the hot Argentinian night. There was even a surprise proposal: Wisson and Van Hereson were getting hitched.

Such was the high drama of snail racing.

Final Classification
1. *Clink* ridden by Atkins (GBR)
2. *Farlingworth* ridden by Ratanang (RSA)
3. *Clyde van Dusen* ridden by Van Hereson (NED)
4. *Waikikamukau* ridden by Wisson (NZL)
5. *Whatshesaid* ridden by Khatri (IND)
6. *Snotstreep* ridden by Meyer (RSA)
7. *Shellton Jr.* ridden by Juma (TZA)
8. *Salty Foam* ridden by Smith (USA)
9. *Condottiere* ridden by Bianchi (ITA)
10. *Caracol Rapido* ridden by Rodríguez (ESP)
11. *Island Raider* ridden by Martin (COK)
12. *Faster Than It Looks* ridden by Musa (NGA)
13. *Local Hero* ridden by Fernandez (ARG)
14. *Pop* ridden by Medvedev (RUS)

DNFs
- *Malchance III* ridden by Chevrolet (FRA)
- *Captain Crunch* ridden by Martin (CAN)
- *Ivory Beauty* ridden by Odhiambo (KEN)
- *Hypnos* ridden by Konstantinopolites (GRC)
- *Patty Cake* ridden by Wagner (DEU)

Other
Timely Journal – 3
Bright Report – 2

TRAVEL: THE PEOPLE OF THE CLOUD
PART I: FILTERIA MAJOR
BY CARMICHAEL CARMICHAEL

The Cloud Islands are a small chain of landmasses dotting the Quadratic Sea. The natives here are not one people. Instead, their cultures changed from island to island, united only by the glittering Quadratic, the tropical climate, and a shared mythology. The latter being a common 'creation story' and a reverence for an entity named "Wife Eye".

In the months I spent in the island chain, I got to know three of these tribes. Navigating my custom-built skiff from landmass to landmass, I spent a few weeks with each. Meeting the locals, partaking in their cuisine, learning a few words of their language, and – finally – saying sorrowful goodbyes.

The first tribe I encountered were the Gramin people of Filteria Major, the northern most island of the chain. Golden beaches, leaning palm trees, and a lush viridian forest greeted me as the hull of the boat hissed onto the shore. The smell of seawater was overtaken by the fertile gaminess of the jungle.

I had only just found my land legs when a flash from the undergrowth caught my eye. There were whispering voices. I secured the boat and shouted a greeting into the wilderness. No response. I greeted the unseen strangers in every language I was equipped with. Still no response.

Movement in the undergrowth – the snap and slap of bodies

running through grass and thick leaves. A flash – and another. Still my words seem to have no effect. I sat down on the sand – showing them that I was no threat. This seemed to do the trick.

Four people emerged. They could not have been older than teenagers. Each clutched a small metallic rectangle – arm outstretched, a point of light shining from the strange item. Traditional weapons of some unusual design, I realized.

I raised my hands and told them that I posed no danger. Their language must have been so beyond mine that verbal communication was of little use.

As they steadily stepped closer, encircling me, I became aware of their traditional dress. Both the males and females (there were two of each) were dressed similarly: blue denim-like pantaloons, and flamboyant shirts printed with palm trees or dolphins. These must have had some cultural significance that I have yet to fathom.

Their rectangles flashed. They nodded to each other. Without warning, they all surrounded what I believed to be the dominant female. They glanced at her rectangle, each making a grunt of approval in turn. It seemed that showing reverence for her secured her favor.

Once this little ritual was concluded, they turned to me. They regarded my clothes (which had become stained and ragged as I paddled here all the way from Portsmouth) and my skiff with rapt curiosity. It seemed likely that I was the first Englishman to wash up on their shores.

"Carmichael," I said thumping my chest.

The strangeness of the Queen's English made them laugh. After a few minutes of confusion, I eventually established that the dominant female was called "Darla". The others made do with simpler names: "Her", "Him", and "Dave". They touched my hair, tugged gently on my shirt, and examined my boat. I presumed that they were checking me for weapons. After I satisfied their search, they took me by the arm and led me into the jungle.

Their village was a dazzling sight. Thatch-roofed houses huddled together in a clearing. The central space was dominated by a metallic tower that stretched into the sky like a giant needle. The outer circumference of the settlement was used for farming (i.e. maize and kale).

The residence gathered as we approached. Each held out a metal rectangle – lights shining. They did not so much speak to each other

– instead, their traditional weapons beeped. The tone and tenor of which conveyed complex meanings that were beyond my comprehension.

I was led to the central tower. Eventually, I learnt that this was a shrine to "Fahivegee" a child of "Wife Eye" specific to this island. It is believed that he watches over the village and helps the people to "really connect".

The crowd gathered to flash their rectangles at me. Some stood beside me while they did so, others kept a safe distance. This is when it became clear that the flashes produced facsimiles of the scene on the surface of the rectangles – much like photographs, but without the limits of film.

Seemingly satisfied that I was no threat, they invited me into one of their huts. There were no tables or chairs – at least not as we know them. One was expected to sit on large colorful sacks filled with soft pebbles. It did nothing for my aching back. The walls were decorated with empty frames and "floating shelves" which were stacked with nonsensical items (rusted bits of metal, empty pots, and small canvases with mandala-like patterns).

The meal of the day was brought in. Their diet appeared to be predominantly vegan – something they chatted about endlessly. Not that I understood a word. The day's offering: sliced pickles on a kale leaf resting on a bed of cauliflower "rice". It was certainly an acquired taste.

The pre-meal ritual involved flashing the plate with your rectangle. It is not entirely clear why this is done. At first, I assumed that they flashed everything they were unsure about. In this case, having your meal prepared entirely by a neighboring tribe can have its risks. My working theory is that, by chronicling his every meal, a tribesman can identify what exactly did him in – should illness arise.

I spent several weeks earning my keep around the village. I tilled the fields, harvested kale, collected dirty laundry, and untangled the Sacred Cables reserved for imparting energy to the rectangles. Gradually, I won their trust. So much so that they began teaching me a few words in their language. Whilst our primary means of communication still relied heavily on hand gestures and animal noises, I was soon able to follow sections of a conversation.

They also revealed the central tenants of their faith to me. While they took pride in personal hygiene and appearance, true nirvana was attained by gaining – what they called – *follows*. This abstract force –

much like karma, luck, or Black Friday deals – guided the behavior of the typical Gramin tribesperson. This not only meant looking the part, but also developing a reverence for the unusual. For follows, a tribesperson would venture to dangerous places on the island (e.g. deep caverns or sheer cliffs) to flash something unique – preferably before anyone else does.

As hours became days, it became easier to distinguish between villagers. There was a mysterious hierarchy that coalesced into social classes. At first, I believed that this was linked to role (i.e. farmer, hut builder, fashion blogger, etc.), but instead it all came down to this abstract force of follows. Everyone made an effort. A farmer would be in the midst of tilling the field for kale planting, when he would stop midway to take a picture with his rectangle. The same strange ritual occurred with every activity. Perhaps as a naive observer, I was blind to its true merits, but it seemed to stifle productivity more than anything else.

But then again, the tribespeople were happy, healthy, and seemingly fulfilled.

Nearly everyone, that is. A dumpy tribesman caught my attention as the days rolled by. While others went about with their rectangles flashing this and flashing that, this young man was never seen with one. I took to calling him Shelby and he became of great interest to me. Sometimes you can learn a lot from outsiders.

My nights were spent in the company of my trusty typewriter. Fresh air and a sky blooming with stars does wonders for writer's anxiety. I filled pages and pages with my observations – my efforts to capture and comprehend the Gramin culture. I was so productive, in fact, that my dwindling paper supply was causing me to worry.

The villagers found the mechanical clack-clack of my typewriter a strange addition to the night-time jungle soundtrack. The shack they kindly lent to me was stuffed with wide-eyed observers for the first few nights. They flashed their rectangles at me, capturing this quaint habit. Some laughed when the bell rang. To others, the act of removing a page from the machine too offensive to the senses.

I held up pages of my writing to show them. Some flashed their rectangles, but none of them seemed to grasp the inky symbols. How strange our modern ways must seem to these people.

Interest soon dwindled. By the end of the first week, I was left alone to my typing – with one exception. Each night the chubby face of Shelby would lean into the shack and cast a curious look at my typewriter. I soon learned that trying to communicate with him would only scare him off. If I ignored him and just focused on my report, he would eventually find a beanbag in a corner to watch me from.

It took me a while to understand his curiosity. There were no words, no gestures – just a glint in his eye. I would know that look anywhere: the boy was suffering from hypergraphia. He needed a pen or pencil in his hands. He had ink in his veins and a strong desire to bleed it onto a page.

How frustrating it must be to want to say something and no means of doing it.

I cranked a fresh page into the typewriter and stepped aside. I tried every gesture I knew to get the idea across. The boy looked at me wide eyed. Trembling, he placed himself behind the typewriter and stared at the blank page. He stared and stared. After an agonizing moment in which he placed and replaced his fingers on the keys, he began pulling at his hair.

Ah, a natural.

I reassured him that it will come in time, but my words and gestures just seemed to anger him. He stomped off back to his hut.

I make several attempts at getting him to write, but with no success. Either the alphabet was something he was still coming to terms with, or he was a misguided believer in 'waiting for inspiration'. Whatever the cause of his reluctance to put word to paper, it was clear that he burned with the need to do so. This became intensely interesting to me – how often does one get a chance to observe a writer in the wild?

While my nights were consumed by watching this young man stare angrily at my typewriter, my days were spent trying to fathom the rest of the village. I attempted to follow a different villager on her or his wanderings. The vast majority of these – I am afraid to say – were rather dull. There were only so many pictures one could take of kale, for instance.

The more dangerous excursions interested me more. I followed villagers to the tops of peaks and the bottoms of canyons. Each time I waited patiently for them to take a *selfish* – a picture with their face included. These puzzled me slightly. It was done in an effort to prove that the photographer was indeed present at the time of taking the photograph – this was the best explanation I could come up with.

There were many examples of logically flawed behavior. For

instance, one bright morning the light was 'just right' for a group picture below the central tower. People were positioned. A photographer was nominated. Several attempts were made.

Eventually they had the composition they required. The result was shared among participants. While they were staring at their rectangles with evident delight, a bright scarlet bird glided over the village. I shouted, pointed, waved my arms wildly, but it was no use. Either they paid little heed to muddy old men or they were utterly lost to the image on their scared idols. Either way, it did not seem like a clever survival strategy to this journalist. For instance, what if the bird was a predatory parrot? Perhaps this was part of their strange urge to be as close to danger as possible.

The magnificent bird – undoubtably a species hitherto undiscovered by ornithologists the world over – glided peacefully over our heads and disappeared into the thick jungle. A majestic sight, to be sure. Moments later they were all wondering why I was out of breath. They went about their day, seemingly satisfied with whatever that last picture was.

Well, perhaps this was not true for every member of the tribe. Our dear Shelby was sitting on his porch staring off into the jungle. Once the villagers scattered, his eyes followed Darla as she and her entourage disappeared into their glittery hut.

That night, Shelby put his first words on paper. The keys were hit with such passionate force, that the words came out mangled and twisted. There was an entire line of exclamation marks. It was yet to reach the level of 'bad', but every writer starts somewhere. Every story is written to chase some need that can never truly be met.

I was proud of dear Shelby. Despite the deplorable state of his first attempt, I nailed the page to my shack wall. It reminded me of my own clumsy efforts to commit my thoughts to paper. I will never forget. Mother and I were crossing the Jordanian desert on the back of a five-legged camel called Bob. We were scouring the sands for a lost Nabatean stonemason's workshop for many days, but with no success. We happened upon a wandering merchant who listed off directions at the speed of a spontaneous sandstorm. Mother instructed me to write it down. In that moment I wanted nothing more than to impress her. Perhaps it was the wonkiness of Bob's pentapedal locomotion, or my inexperience with a crayon (I was only four), but my handwriting was anything but neat. Mother said that it was fine as long as I could understand what the squiggles meant. Her words have stayed with me to this day.

I shared this sentiment with Shelby, but – alas – my words meant nothing to the youngster. I keep this page with me still.

Eventually the time came to move on. I gathered my things and gestured 'goodbye' with waves and handshakes. The entire village followed me to my skiff which was – by now – covered in fallen palm leaves and filled with beach sand. They flashed their rectangles at me as I cleared the mess.

Once the boat was set free and pushed to the water's edge, I pulled out the creased map of the Quadratic Sea. I pointed at Filteria Major. This was met with nods, grunts, and the flash of a rectangle. It seemed that they understood that the blob of green was their island. I pointed to the next island in the chain. The huddled villagers shook their heads collectively.

From their grunts, gestures, and blurry pictures, I understood that this island – Hearin Island – was home to a tribe of people who communicated solely via pre-recorded messages. Their customary greeting – which chilled the blood of even the most fearsome islander – went something like *"Sorry for the voice note"*.

I pointed to the next island. Everyone nodded at this. The island was called Soft Stone and was home to a tribe that was *"heavy into meditation"*. There was consensus that this was a peaceful place to visit.

I loaded my typewriter, crinkled paper, sleeping bag, bag of kale, and remaining toilet paper rations into the boat. I turned back to the tribe to see them looking at me expectantly. They handed me a gift. Placed in a decorative bag – for they had not discovered the ways of gift wrapping – was my very own rectangle. I thanked them as best as I could, but I hardly knew what to do with the thing. However, it had a nice edge to it – perhaps I could use it to strip bark or even strike sparks to light a fire.

I pushed the boat off and watched Filteria Major recede. One or two villagers waved, most flashed their rectangles, but Shelby – who finally made his appearance – stared forlornly. Perhaps I should have taken him with me, but then again, that was not really my place.

I waved. He waved back. That is when I made up my mind to say one final goodbye to the boy before returning home.

My back ached from paddling. All that time I spent doing minimal manual labor made my muscles lazy. But I soldiered on. I put my head down and paddled with all my might. Much like the

Gramin tribespeople, I became so engrossed in my own activity that I failed to notice my surroundings. As such, it came as rather a large surprise when a fishing net fell upon me.

To be continued...

MOTORING: REVIEWING THE LETHE SERIES D HATCHBACK
BY JAMISON JEFFERSON JONES

I am a man of the people.
    Certainly, I review the rarest and most exclusive cars in the world. But I cannot and should not be mistaken for an elite – someone who thinks himself above everyone else. Evidently, merely stating this was not enough to convince my boss, Mr Balding, that there was no need to change the kinds of cars I reviewed.
    Enter the Lethe Series D Hatchback economy car. Anything but elite or exclusive. It certainly was not rare either, as the Invocorp factory is, apparently – even as you read this – pumping out hundreds of the damn things.
    It was my job to review it.
    This was some form of punishment. Either my readership was starting to see me as "out of touch" or the Bright Report was still covering the cost of the Maserati I (through no true fault of my own) dinged last month. However, it was more likely that the readership of the Report has gone from the "Joneses" to the "Man on the Street". If this is the case – welcome, new reader, and remember to have a dictionary handy.
    My drive would take place on a cloudy Wednesday. I was not in the best frame of mind, as wife number three and I had a smidgen of a fight.
    It happens.
    The driver from the factory announced his arrival with a honk. I was picking my socks and underpants from the rosebush at the time.

I waved at him with as much amicability as one could muster with one's newly aired laundry over one's shoulder.

The man – a neatly combed individual in a neat lab coat – waved back sheepishly. His bespectacled eyes scanned the debris littering the front lawn. The flatscreen, which was resting in a nest of the glittering remains of the lounge window, caught his eye.

He was about to speak – he wanted to say the polite thing, to postpone the drive to a more convenient time. I did not give him the chance. I rushed up to him and exchanged my pile of clothes for the car keys.

"Thank you," I said. He gave me a questioning look. "Oh, just leave it in a hedge somewhere, there's a good man."

I glanced down the street – where was the damn…oh yes, he parked it here.

Some lesser publications label the new Lethe with lofty words like "innovative" or "game-changer". These publications are all wrong. There is nothing innovative about the car – it is almost too ordinary, too generic. If I had not seen the man park it, I would not have been able to find it. It faded into the background like a vegan at a spit roast.

Well, here goes.

The doors were manually unlocked – no clicker, no industry standard remote access. This was old school. I unlocked the old-fashioned door which was flimsy – so much so, that I worried that I would bend it if I pulled at the wrong angle. The interior was as perfectly beige as a plain slice of bread.

Even the steering wheel is a boring circular shape. It is my belief that the committee – for it was most certainly designed by one – sat in a beige boardroom somewhere and decided to save on the creativity side of the car-building business. The car almost looked like a child's drawing: the classic rectangle upon a longer rectangle with wheels vaguely beneath it all.

The Lethe is boring.

In the realm of supercars, the moment of turning the ignition ignites a passion in even the most frigid petrol head. Words like 'purr' or 'roar' are often placed upon the sound of the engine spinning into life. With the Lethe, words like 'splutter' or 'cough' over did it – it was more like Bessy's final breath before she was loaded into the abattoir van.

I worked the flimsy pedals and placed the car in reverse. The head of the stick shift was worryingly loose. What passed for a handbrake in the Lethe would be counted as a collapsible umbrella handle anywhere else. The rear-view was no more than a shiny mirror sticker – not even glass. The breaks were spongy – the sun visors moved when the vehicle came to an abrupt stop.

This was a bad start.

I waved at lab coat man as I chittied down the street. It was time to open her up.

I live in the country. I like occasionally disrupting the rural idyl with the roar of an Italian engine or the screeching of tires. It reminded the neighbors of my presence and kept the local sheep population on their hoof-tips. Alas, the Lethe had no such impact on the environment. Folk snoozed in their beds and the sheep grazed gormlessly – none noticing the little car bump its way down the hilly country roads.

Before I even left town, the sun visor and I were mortal enemies. With every gearshift and every minor bump that rocked the car's wooden suspension, the damn thing flapped down to obscure my view. Fortunately, I was not going fast enough to hit something (or, at least, fatally hit something), but I think I missed my turning.

I had hoped to test the Lethe in the city streets – it was what it was built for, after all. However, thanks to this thing blocking my view every few yards, I was headed deeper into the countryside. I had never been down this road before – I never had a reason to sightsee the local…whatever else there was in the country. Milking sheds? Grain fields? Families with uncomfortably small and circular gene pools?

The Lethe and I were headed into the unknown.

It is also worth pointing out that the wind hissed through the doorframes when one got up to speed. The latter phrase conjures imagery of a car hurtling along a stretch of road, putting its aerodynamics and handling to the test. Sadly, the Lethe probably never saw the inside of a wind tunnel – the gale would surely flatten the poor thing like one of my wife's soufflés. That, and we are only doing about 30 miles per hour. The hissing would drive anyone mad.

I came to a fork in the road. The signs were of little use. To the left was "Town Centre" with no indication of what town specifically. Perhaps it was one of those signs that filtered out outsiders. To the right was "Tupman Dell" – an equally unhelpful label. I stood there for a few minutes, weighing my options.

A sheep in an adjoining field was giving me a meaningful look. Normally the things would scatter at the sound of an engine, but this clunky trap must have seemed less intimidating than a lawnmower.

I pulled out my phone. Blast – no reception, no GPS.

The idle vibrations made the sun visor flap down again. Alright, there was only one thing for it: I had seen enough of the car to write a review, now it was time to go home. The strip of road between the stone walls was narrow, but the Lethe could surely manage a basic three-point turn.

I put it into gear and heard the engine roar. I stared at the dash in disbelief. The revs were fine. The throttle had not been touched, but the sound grew louder. It was not the Lethe – it was an enormous green tractor bearing down on me. The sheep made a break for it. The massive contraption rolled up to the back of me and the driver – a rotund figure in suspenders – lent on his horn.

I climbed out, hoping to explain the situation and to ask for some directions. The horn beeped and beeped. Perhaps he hoped that the harder he pressed the damn thing, the faster I would move. He was red faced.

"I'm terribly sorry," I said in my most cordial tone. I am a man of the people, after all.

The humpty dumpty man leaned out of the cabin. There was a most fearsome expression of impatience on his face. "Well?" he barked. "Are yeh movin' or what? 'Aven't got all day. Dah I look like I 'ave all day?"

Honestly, the man looked as if he was between cardiac arrests, so he probably did not have all hour.

Why are countryfolk so unpleasant? I did not imagine that I would spend the morning chatting with tractor drivers and exchanging glances with a sheep. I just wanted to go home. There was no hiding in the car. The Lethe would provide no hinderance whatsoever to the tractor should the man decide to proceed. It should therefore be noted that the car has a negative three on the Intimidation Factor – if there was such a thing. I shrank back into the driver seat and the engine mumbled into life.

No turning back. Town Centre or Tupman Dell – those were the only options. The sun visor flapped down and made the decision for me: there must be a shop in town somewhere that sells duct tape or similar.

I put the car in gear amid a chorus of tractor honks and puttered towards the left. Mercifully, the fat man went to the right. I could breathe again. I could think again. My mission was simple: secure the blasted visor and rattle on back home. However, the thought of picking up the row again turned my insides. Perhaps a slow walk about town – whatever town it was – would do me some good. I could meet a local or two. Surely they would be more agreeable than the man in the tractor.

That way I could kill a flock of birds with one stone: (1) buy duct tape, (2) finish the drive, (3) give Deborah time to cool off, and (4) show Mr Balding that I am, indeed, in touch with ordinary people.

Easy, right? But little did I know...

The road wound its way to a small town on a hill surrounded by lush green fields. It had an old town feel: stone buildings, narrow streets, and narrower shops. All in all, it looked rather fancy. Perhaps I could bring wife number three here once things have calmed down.

There was what passed as a supermarket near the center of the hodgepodge of buildings. It was busier than I would have thought for such a small town, but I found a parking soon enough. I clambered out, stretched, and felt several vertebrae click. I am not a short man by most standards. As such, I could not imagine being scrunched up in the Lethe for a long drive. No matter how I positioned the beige seats, I would never be comfortable.

I manually locked the door and wandered into the grocery store. The place was bustling with locals. The crowd consisted of grown men in shorts – despite the chilly bite in the air – and hard-warn women in overalls. The odd nuclear family dotted the place too – bossy mothers, grumpy husbands, and rowdy children. I hate shopping.

There were several stands of fresh produce. Several banners and flags proclaimed them to be locally produced. Some even had labels with custom mascots – a corn man, a sheep with a monocle, etc. – that looked like the best efforts of the local graphic designer. You know the sort: a lanky twentysomething with a goiter and a lack of female companionship.

I had to get out of this place. The longer I stayed, the more 'down to earth' I felt – something that could only come off after a long, steamy shower in my designer bathroom.

I slinked down the DIY aisle. Just my luck – it was occupied. I was there for merely a millisecond when a young woman accosted me with a tray of greyish liquid.

"Energy drink?" she inquired.

I dismissed her with a wave of a hand. I did not have time for this nonsense.

"Hey, I've seen you before, mister," she said. "Come on. You look thirsty."

Where was the damned duct tape? The girl shadowed me down the aisle despite my lack of interest. I must admit that she did not look like the typical shop sample girl. Usually, they were in a uniform of some description, right? Not all in black with a wide-brimmed hat stuck with feathers. Perhaps Halloween came early.

"No thank you," I said. "I'm just here for tape."

"Hold this," she said handing me the entire tray of samples. "You mean like this?" Holding her hat in one hand and stretching out with the other, she unhooked a roll of industrial duct tape. It was the only one they had.

"Yes, thank you," I said holding out the tray.

She held up the roll like a monocle. A bright blue eye studied me. "Will that be all, mister?" she asked. "Only, you look hassled. Very." Something caught her gaze behind me. "Oops. Got to go! Drink up." She turned and hurried down the aisle, tape in hand.

I was about to pursue when a beleaguered woman in a tracksuit blocked my way. "Just one per customer," she said and tore the tray from me. Greyish liquid sloshed in the plastic shot glasses.

I mumbled a confused apology. "Umm…do you have any more duct tape?" I asked her. She gave an exasperated sigh and stormed off with her tray. I stood there for a moment – dazed.

Where did the girl run off to? She could not have gone far. I rushed down the aisle and scanned the tills. No black hat. What had just happened?

This really did not matter. All I cared about in that moment was to get home. Damn the sun visor – there must me some way I can remove it entirely. Damn this little village and their weirdly dressed shoplifters – keep the tape, what do I care? Damn the fight at home – even if I had to wade into it again, it was better than being helpless in the middle of nowhere.

I exited the grocery store. A realization dawned on me as I stomped through the parking lot.

Where was the car? I parked it near the end, here – I am sure of it. How hard could it be to spot a boring rectangular car? What color was the damned thing again? I waved the keys in vain – there was no button to press, there were no indicators to guide me. I walked up and down the car park, hoping that the arrival and departure of cars would give me a clue. No such luck.

Perhaps some unlucky fool stole the car. I glanced down the adjoining streets, hoping to catch sight of a puttering little vehicle. If someone had left with it, they could not have gotten far – at least, not in such a short space of time.

I slunk back to the grocery. Perhaps a security camera caught something. This is when I caught sight of something else: a black hat with black feathers. My duct tape thief was peering into a trolley – one that she clearly was not the owner of. Said owner was a distracted mother of three trying to keep her children in tow. While the mother was admonishing her son for dropping his toy car down a grate, the girl was rummaging through the bags.

I had to act. "Stop! You!"

The girl, the mother, and the three children looked up at my approach. The girl backed away from the trolley slightly.

"There you are," she said. "I've been looking for you all over. Did you like the energy drink? Booster ten thousand or something like that, right?"

The mother and children looked from the girl to my confused expression and back again.

"My dad," said the girl rolling her eyes. "He gets confused sometimes. Very. But you do what you can."

I was not sure what part of that insulted me most. "I beg your pardon?"

"Right," said the mother. She placed a consoling hand on the girl's shoulder. "I do know. I know he appreciates it – even if he doesn't always show it." She turned back to her children. "Come along. Sorry, Sam, I'll get you another car. That one is going to the sea."

The four of them ventured into the car park. The boy – the one that had lost his toy car – stared at me through his tears. He could not have been more than ten, eleven – something like that. He pulled on his mother's blouse and pointed at me.

"That's, that's…" he began.

"Not now, Sam."

I turned my suspicious gaze on the shoplifter. "What did you take?" I asked holding out my hand.

She raised hers. "Take? Nothing at all." She smiled brightly at me.

"How about you? You look like you've lost something."

"Yes," I hissed. "My duct tape. What happened to it? You left me standing there with the juice."

She suppressed a laugh. "Oh, the tape?" She scratched her chin. "It wasn't what I was looking for, so I just put it on some random shelf." Her eyes narrowed. "What did you need it for, anyway? I've never seen anyone so desperate for the stuff. Got someone tied up in a trunk or something?"

"What?" This woman was infuriating. "No. In fact, I'm looking for my car I can't…I can't remember where I parked it."

"Oh dear, oh dear," she said. The feathers flapped as she shook her head. "Guess my little fib was closer to the truth than…"

"I'm not losing my mind," I said. "And I'm not old. Now if you'll excuse me." I pushed past her. There must be someone here who could help me. Security maybe.

The girl followed me as I pushed my way through the crowd of shoppers. "Hey, that little boy recognized you. Are you famous or what?"

"I review cars," I said flatly. I scanned the field of heads.

"Ah, that explains some of it," she said. "Do you usually lose the cars you review?"

"No," I said through gritted teeth. "Excuse me," I said addressing one of the till ladies. "Do you have a security chap or something. Only, my car appears to have been stolen."

Before she could answer, the customer unpacking his groceries onto the conveyer piped up. "Oi! It's my turn. Get in line."

The till woman shrugged and went on scanning.

"Melody Lime," said my feather-hatted acquaintance. It certainly sounded made up. Of course, what self-respecting shoplifter would tell the truth to the man of the fourth estate.

"I didn't ask," I said. I pushed past her and went to the next till point.

"It's no use," she said cheerfully. "People 'round here won't steal cars. No one will help."

I rounded on her. "I beg your pardon," I said. "I caught you rummaging through that person's shopping. How could I believe that people here don't steal?"

She raised her hands in surrender again. "Like I said: I didn't take anything. Especially not from Antonia Weller. She doesn't have anything to take."

I shook my head and pushed my way out of the shop. I patted my pants pocket...my empty pants pocket. A cold feeling bloomed in the pit of my stomach.

Melody walked up to me. Her brilliant blue eyes look at me as if she were studying my form for sculpture. "You look like you've seen a ghost."

"My phone," I said. "I left it in the car." I glanced about the parking lot with wild desperation. It must be here somewhere. I was in the middle of nowhere without a means of transportation and no contact with the outside world. I felt like Mr Carmichael on one of his rugged adventures. Only, I was not built for that. God, what am I going to do?

"Mister? Are you listening to me?" said Melody. She waved a hand in front of my face. She had to stand on her tiptoes to reach. "Maybe I can find your house," she said. "I'm sure I've seen you before. You live in a brick house."

"All the houses are brick!" I said. Sanity was departing.

"Not all," she said thoughtfully. "But yours is bricky. Very. Glass all on the one side, I think."

I ignored her. "This is just great," I said to the parking lot at large. "I'm lost in the middle of...where is this...Kent? No means of getting home. No phone. God, my wife is going to have all the more reason to leave me. I can't even review a stupid, damn..." I trailed off. "This would have never happened if they gave me a real car. Not that stupid..."

Melody snapped her fingers. "I have an idea," she said.

"No! No ideas. What do you want from me, girl?" I was going to blow something. I could feel the blood rushing through my brain. "Don't you have something better to do! Go away."

She shrugged. "Not really that busy," she said cheerfully. "I can help you out, I think."

"How can you possibly do that?"

"You said you do cars, right?" she asked.

I felt a bit deflated. "Yes," I said softly. "I review them. I've reviewed thousands. Millions of readers around the globe know and trust my opinion on the world's best – and sometimes slightly overrated – cars." I fell to my knees.

"Right," she said. She scrunched up her eyes. "So, at a stretch, you know how they work."

"I suppose," I said meekly.

"Perfect." She righted her hat. "Come along then." She hooked an arm under mine and – with some effort – got me to my feet. "Come on then," she said walking off.

Dazed and slightly embarrassed, I followed her.

"Where are we going?"

"Home," she said. "Well, in a sort of roundabout way."

I gave one final look at the car park. I still could not see the Lethe Series D Hatchback economy car. Either it had been stolen or the thing was so unremarkable that it erased itself from reality. How had things come to this? Days that start with fights are never ordinary days. Now look, I am following a stranger into the unknown. A total stranger dressed like a witch. Morticia in a sunhat.

We walked and walked through the village. There seemed to be little logic in the directions Melody was taking: first down a main road, then down an alley, then down some strange byway that seemed to be nothing but a gap in someone's fence. She seemed at home with these unusual routes. I, on the other hand, was not known for my walking.

The further we went, the more lost I became. A voice in the back of my mind told me that I was being led to my doom.

"Listen," I said as we crossed someone's wild back garden. "I don't have my wallet on me or anything."

"Okay?"

"So, if you're thinking of robbing me…"

She giggled as she climbed onto a crate. "We have to jump the fence here," she said. She caught my horrified expression. "Relax," she said. "You just need to get out more. This is the fastest way, trust me."

I had no choice – I had come so far. We clambered over two more fences and emerged in a cornfield. We followed a snaking path through the tall stalks. I was not sure how she could tell one turn from another. After what seemed like an eternity, we cleared the field and reached a fence. The glittering tarmac of a road greeted us.

"Left or right," I asked. "Which one would get me home? Or a bus stop, at least." The thought of public transport usually made me queasy, but my feet were killing me. Needs must.

Melody pointed straight across the road to the opposite field. There, beyond a wooden fence were rolling grassland populated with several large horses.

"Any good with horses?" she asked.

"No," I said. "Cars – not horses."

She giggled. "I know." She climbed over the fence. Her sleeve caught on a splinter and tore. "Darn," she said examining the rip. "Fix it later. Come on. We're almost there." She went right. I could not tell you which cardinal direction we were headed or if it was closer or further from home.

"Are you sure?" I asked as I followed.

"Yeah, the farm is just up here," she said cheerfully.

"Farm? I don't live on a farm!"

"Of course not, stupid," she said. It became clear to me that my every utterance was a source of great comedy for her. What common company have I found myself in? "No one said it's your farm," she said. "Come on, walk faster. Black gets hot in the sun. Very. Can't keep waiting for you. Chop-chop."

I felt dizzy as I plodded on behind her. This is what a mental breakdown feels like, I thought. I thought I could keep my life together with just another silly car review and thereafter things would be better. Or, at least, the same as always. But things had become miraculously worse.

"The horses belong to mister Wardle," she continued conversationally. I found it hard to care. "He's itching to buy out all the surrounding farms, you know. Bit of baddin if you ask me. His offers are woefully slim – not even desperate families can afford to take the bag of change he's offering. So, instead, he terrorizes his neighbors, hoping to force them out. He even starts fires, but there's no real proof. But there was this one time when I saw…"

"Why are you telling me this?"

She shrugged. "Thought it was relevant since we were walking past. Thought you like understanding things."

"What makes you think I care about insignificant local dramas?" I shot. "I just want to go home."

She nodded, feathers flapping. "Soon, soon. Oh, look," she pointed towards a group of low buildings I took for stables. Standing beside them was a shiny green tractor.

"I've seen that contraption," I said. "It's the bugger that bore down on me and honked like a deranged goose."

"That will be mister Wardle then," she said with a smile. "Come on. Almost there."

She said that our intended destination was the next farm over. It sounded like a brief walk by her description. However, it was dawning on me that this strange woman had no concept of direction or distance. It felt like an eternity before we reached the end of Mr Wardle's estate. I was near collapse for my body was adapted to the rigors of long drives and high-speed corners – not low-level parkour and cross-country jaunts.

We turned down a long gravel drive. The crunching pebbles made my ears ache.

"None of this looks like home," I moaned.

Melody pointed ahead at an overgrown farmhouse. It seemed lopsided, as if the wind blew only from one side and the walls paid the price.

"We'll get help here," she said. "This is the Weller farm." She went on to describe the family in alarming detail. The father went missing overseas, leaving Antonia Weller to look after Sam (11), Mary (8), and Anne (4) by herself. The place was a pomegranate farm that had been in the family for generations. It ensured that the family and their employees had a steady income for a while. However, since Flamingo Industries placed their Instant Powdered Pomegranate Cups™ on the market, things have taken a down swing. With the bills adding up and the staff dismissed, Antonia was thinking of taking a tiny cheque from Mr Wardle.

"Again, what does any of this have to do with me?" I asked. "I'm just a car guy."

We had reached the front door by now. I could hear conversation from within. Melody shrugged at me and then promptly rang the doorbell.

"You'll see," she whispered. "Or you won't. I'm not sure about you yet."

The door opened before I could say anything else. Antonia opened the door, blowing a strand of hair from her face. I realized that she was the woman with the trolley.

"Good morning – or afternoon, I see," she said. Her eyes went from Melody's hat to my face. "Oh, hello. You and your dad. How can I help you?"

"I'm not –"

"My dad is a mechanic," Melody cut in. "He brought many an engine back from the rusty grave. He's here to help."

Antonia seemed to take a moment to register what the girl said. "How did you…"

"It's 'round back, right?" Melody continued.

"Umm...yes," she said. There was a commotion in the kitchen. It seemed the children were having some trouble unpacking the groceries. She was fighting the urge to run back to them. "Yes, out back," she said. "But I can't..."

"No charge," said Melody quickly. "We just need to use your phone to call a taxi once we're finished."

One of the children called from the kitchen. They seemed like a nightmare – luckily, none of my relationships ever went in that direction.

"Okay, but..."

"You go look after them," said Melody. "We'll sort things. I'll call you when we're done."

A little face peered round the crack. It was the boy that lost his car. "Mommy," he said. "Thought you said we can have all these sweets and icky veggies and whole bunch of..."

"Yes, dear," said Antonia. "Like I said, I don't know how we got those – we certainly didn't pay for them. Don't worry about that now, Sam. Come say hello."

The boy stepped out onto the stoep and half-hid behind his mother's leg. "Hello," he said softly.

"This nice man and his daughter are here to fix Henry," she said. "I'm sorry, sir, what's your name?"

Before I could answer, the boy blurted out: "Jamison Jefferson Jones – he does the car stuff, mommy."

"Umm...yes," I said. "But don't tell anyone."

Antonia looked at me with an expression of total incomprehension. "Well, I guess I can count my lucky stars that I have the services of a renowned mechanic. And all for the price of a phone call."

"Very lucky," said Melody smiling broadly.

A glass shattered in the kitchen. Antonia pinched the bridge of her nose. "Alright," she sighed. "Sam, please unlock the barn for mister Jones. I'll go help your sisters before we have to sieve our dinner."

Following Sam, we traipsed around the house. It was ringed by rows upon rows of evenly spaced pomegranate trees. The branches were bursting with bright red fruits. The spicy-fruity smell was thick in the air.

"Where's your car, mister Jones?" asked Sam as we walked. He was clutching a chipped model of a Lamborghini Countach.

"It's at home," I said. Technically, this was the truth.

"He decided to walk today," said Melody cheerfully. "You go ahead. I'm going to take a little walk up the hill."

She disappeared into the grove before I could say a word.

The boy led me to the barn behind the house. It was just as misshapen as the rest of the house. The door creaked a horror-movie note as it opened. Rusty farming equipment glinted in the light. Sunbeams lanced through holes in the roof planks and lit motes of dust in golden light. It was an altar to agriculture and amid it all was a rusty tractor.

"You must be Henry," I said.

"Yes," said the kid. "Are you sure you can fix him? He hasn't worked in a while." He looked up at me with doubt glinting in his dark eyes. "Only you didn't do much of that when you had a show."

It felt like there was a bag of ice in my stomach. "No, not on the show," I admitted. "But that wasn't my role. I've worked on cars before."

The boy narrowed his eyes. He was onto me. I knew because I had seen this look before, but never in someone that was not related to me by blood or marriage. Determined to prove him wrong, I meaningfully strode towards the rusted machine. I opened the side panel – crusty hinges squealed. Bits of dirt flaked off to reveal a once-bright blue body.

"Alright," I sighed. "I'll have a look in here. You stay close by and hand me any tools I might need."

Worry replaced the doubt in the boy's eyes – another look I knew all too well.

"Don't you worry," I said trying to muster a smile. "I've been asked for tools by many a great mechanic. I promise that I won't shout like they did."

Sam gripped his toy car a little tighter. I should have kept my mouth shut, I guess.

"I suppose some of their greatness must have rubbed off on me," I said. I hoped. I peered into the dark tangle of engine parts and tubes. It looked awfully complicated. Please be something simple, I prayed to the merciless gods of the internal combustion engine.

"Right," I said after a moment. "Where's your toolbox?" I looked up to see Sam already holding it. He placed it down heavily next to me.

"Lots of stuff in there," he said. "And it's easy to reach. So, you don't have to ask."

"Right." Never thought of that one.

Sam cleared a space for himself on a counter and sat, legs dangling.

"I'll never forget my first car," I said. "Called it Jessica – it seems so silly naming a car."

"And after a girl," Sam sneered. "Henry is a better name."

"I suppose. It used to belong to my dad. It was old, clunky, full of rust. Definitely wasn't perfect by any stretch of the imagination, but that didn't make me love it any less. That car was everything to me. Freedom mostly. Responsibility – sure. With every part that broke on it – and trust me, nearly every part did – I learnt more and more about cars. I grew to love the smell of them – the sound – the feeling of speed and control – everything. You're the master of your own destiny when you sit behind the wheel."

"What if you're stuck in traffic?" asked Sam legs kicking.

This made me laugh. "Quite right," I said. "Guess a car teaches you a lot about destiny, then. There's always something to fix – something to maintain – something to…" I trailed off once I saw Melody leaning against the door. She was wearing a smug smile along with her feathered hat.

"Fixed it?" she asked.

"Haven't figured out what's wrong with it," I said.

"Well, you better hurry," she said. "We need to go stage three."

"Stage three?"

"You'll see," she said. She turned to Sam. "Are you keeping an eye on him, Captain?"

The boy nodded.

"Good, coz he gets confused. Very," she said. "He doesn't even know where he parked his car."

I shot her a look.

"I lost my car too," said the boy.

"That's alright," said Melody. "Henry is pretty cool. I'm sure he'll be a big help to you and your mom come harvest season, hey?"

The boy shrugged. "He used to be blue," he said.

I spent several minutes examining the engine with the torch. Unfortunately, it was not as simple as sparkplugs or battery – at least not as far as I could tell. I spent the time naming each of the parts for the boy and giving him a brief – and to the best of my limited knowledge – description of the function of each.

"Well, at least you'll know where everything is then," I said. "Then you can make an informed decision that can benefit everyone."

"You mean, we have to sell Henry?" asked the boy. He was standing next to me, peering closely at the mangled mess that was the engine.

"Oh dear," said another voice. Antonia appeared with a tray clinking with teacups. "That sounds like bad news."

"I'll say," said Melody who was bringing up the rear with a tray of biscuits. The two girls were right behind her staring at her hat.

"I'm really sorry," I said. "I usually drive cars, not fix them."

"Told you he gets confused," said Melody.

"Oh dear," said Antonia. "Never mind, it was sweet of you to look at it for free – and in your condition."

"Don't mention it," I said deflated.

"I won't hear it, I'll call the taxi anyway," said Antonia handing us each a cup of tea. "Won't have you walking all the way home."

"Nah," said Melody. "Walking is good for the brain. We'll let someone in the village know to come and have a look. Dad's got many good contacts – younger contacts."

I should have ended the charade right there, but the tea was hitting the spot. Why complicate things now. After some brilliant homemade biscuits, Melody and I went on our way.

"I'm sorry about…Henry," I said as I followed Melody down an aisle of trees. "I think it's the age and the fact that it stood for so long, and…"

"I knew that it was a long shot," said Antonia. She eyed the ripening red bulbs dangling from the branches. The rich smell was inescapable. "It would have helped with harvesting," she said. "But in the end, people don't really want the fresh stuff anymore."

We said our goodbyes.

"What is stage three?" I asked as we ascended a hill. "Does it involve me going home?"

"You'll see," she said.

We squeezed through a gap in a chain-link fence and ignored several warnings on the creative fates that would befall trespassers. Open fields thundering with horses were on all sides.

"Mr Wardle's property, I presume?"

"Yes," she said. "It's almost the end now."

We heard the distant roar of an engine. Yes, a roar – not a splutter or a wheeze. This was the sound of several cylinders firing. The engine revved. Somewhere in the huddle of farm buildings ahead of us, tires squealed. The sound was magnificent…although.

"That will be mister Wardle heading into town," said Melody.

"Do you hear that?" I asked. "Sounds like a dicky fuel injector or carburetor or something."

She gave me a surprised look. "Yet, no luck with the tractor?"

"Sometimes you can hear that something is wrong," I said.

"So, it's all about listening," she said. "That's remarkable. Very."

"Are you making fun of me?"

"You'll hear if something's wrong," she said. She stuck her tongue out at me. "Come on, he won't be gone long." She picked up the pace.

"I hope you're not thinking of running," I said. "I don't do running. I don't normally do trespassing either, come to think of it."

"And yet?" she said.

"What are we doing here exactly?"

"You are standing guard," she said. "I'm going to have a look inside."

"I'm not sure that I want to be party to this," I said.

"Noted," she said. "Just a quick question: do you know what love is?"

The question took me by surprise. "Well," I started unsure of the words. "It's being there for another person. You're ready and willing to receive all their anxieties and stresses. It's being there no matter how unfair it is that you're the focus of their outside frustrations. Something like that."

She smiled. "I'll take that as a no."

"I've loved cars," I said.

"Ew," she said.

Eventually we reached the stables. The Warble house was multistoried and opulently adorned in concrete sculptures of horses and scantily clad women. Here I use 'opulent' to its most grotesque extent. I was instructed to wait by the entrance to what looked like a shipping container repurposed to be an office. The padlock securing it did not trouble Melody and her hairpin.

"I didn't see that," I said.

"No," she said distractedly. "But I hope you see everything else. Look over there." She pointed to the tractor. It was a monster of a thing – loudly quiet, just sitting there.

The container doors squeaked, and Melody disappeared inside. I stood in the sun feeling exposed. I also realized that I was not at all fond of the smell of horses. My heart raced as I jumped at every sound. I did not fancy the wrath of the humpy dumpy man should he make an unexpected return.

"Come look!" Melody's voice bounced off the metal walls.

I peered in – not wanting to set foot in the formally locked space. There was a desk pilled with paperwork, a dusty fan, and a dented filing cabinet. Furniture you would expect in an office space. But Melody was standing deeper in the container. There, crammed in the end, were several red barrels, a few jerrycans, and four wine bottles. The latter were filled purple-bronze liquid and were stopped with pieces of cloth.

"Pity you don't have your phone," said Melody. "A picture would be helpful. Very."

"You don't have one?"

She shook her head, hat feathers flapping.

I could not help stepping into the space – curiosity got the better of me. The strewn documents were unsigned contracts and land deeds.

"How did you know?" I asked.

She shrugged. "Lucky guesses. Anyway, time for phase four." She held up a set of keys in answer.

A moment later we were rattling down the gravel access road with Mr Wardle's tractor. Despite my protests, Melody was the one driving. I was standing in the high-side trailer and clinging onto the grate for all my life was worth.

"Where to now, exactly?" I asked. "The police?"

"Nah," said Melody. We turned onto the main road. "They can't be bothered. It's like I told you: people don't believe that these things can happen in this town. No luck there."

"Then where?"

"I'm taking you home," she said. She took off her hat and clamped it between her knees.

Home? Home at last. I felt the pit in my stomach again.

"Look," I said. I was blinking against the wind. "I don't know why I'm telling you this, but I'm not eager to go home."

"What? You wanted nothing else a moment ago."

"Yes, yes, I know," I said. I had to shout over the roar of the engine. Sheep scattered as we rolled by. "The thing is: the wife and

I had a bit of a fight. I didn't leave it in the best place this morning so…"

"So," she said. "Fix it."

"It's not that simple."

"It's just like fixing a car," she said. "There's always something to fix – something to maintain – something to…what was it?"

"Care for," I said. "I don't agree. People don't work like cars. My marriage doesn't work like that."

"That's lucky. Very," she said. "Because I don't think you could fix it then."

"I think you're undermining your own point," I said. "But I think I know what you mean."

"Good," she said. We lurched forward as she manhandled the tractor into the next gear. "Then what will you do?"

"Try to fix it," I said.

"And if you can't?"

"I don't know," I admitted.

"Well, at least you'll know where everything is then," she said. "Then you can make an informed decision that can benefit everyone."

I shook my head. "What are you exactly?"

She shrugged. "A force of pure chaos. Something like that." She giggled. "Here we are."

We pulled around a corner and lo, there it was, my house.

I climbed off the trailer slightly dazed. It is funny how small my house looked then. It had appeared so large and unhappy this morning. Certainly, the lounge window was still broken, the flatscreen still stared blindly into the sky. But there was something odd – something new.

"But…," I began. "It wasn't far at all."

"Yeah," she said with a smile. She placed her hat back on. "You were basically lost in your own neighborhood. Told you I've seen you before."

"But…," I spluttered. She was right. Mr Wardle was practically my neighbor.

"Just retrace your steps," she said. "I'm sure you'll find…"

I waved her into silence. "Yes, yes. I don't really care about the thing. I'm going to give it a terrible review anyway."

She looked at me with those deep eyes again. "Does that mean you care about other things now?"

I ignored the insinuation. I could not meet her gaze. Instead, I studied the big green tractor. "Are you going to give it back?"

"Someone will probably track it down at some point," she said with a smile. "Or maybe not. It needs a new coat of paint, don't you think? Blue would do nicely." She glanced up the road.

I was getting the measure of Melody Lime. "Say hello to Mrs Weller for me," I said. It felt like a foolish thing to say.

Melody smiled at me. "Never you mind that," she said nodding towards the house. "You've got your own things to repair." She restarted the tractor and rumbled down the road.

I watched her go. She was an enigma. I wondered back to the house, picking up bits of clothing as I went. It was time to do a whole lot of listening.

Note to the Editor

Dear Mr Balding,

It is not my place to tell you your business, but I have a possible lead on a story for you. Two stories, maybe. Firstly, someone at the crime desk might be interested in evidence concerning an unsolved arson case in my area. This may be a matter for the local police, but as things have come to a standstill, I suspect the Bright Report can light a fire under to spur things on. Secondly, this is not the first time that Flamingo Industries have flooded the market with a dubious GMO product. Either this is a job for Ms. Shánzé at the political desk, or Mr Far at the technology desk – this is, of course, at your discretion. Either way, there are things worth investigating.

As for me, I will be taking my overdue vacation leave. Deborah and I are taking a ramble through the countryside. I think it is time that we take an interest in local affairs.

P.S. Please let me know if you and Ernest would like some pomegranates.

Best regards,
Jameson Jefferson Jones

Note to Mr Jones

Dear Mr Jones,

Thank you for your letter and for your piece. Good work. Better than usual, in fact. A man from Invocorp is eager to have the Lethe returned to him as soon as possible. Perhaps scouting the parking lot after closing time would aid you in tracking the vehicle down. Do let me know as soon as is convenient.

As for your leads – they are very much appreciated.

Unfortunately, Ms. Chánté Shánzé is still missing as of the writing of this letter. Mr Wellington Far is currently doing an important story on toasters. In any case, we will get someone on it as soon as we can.

As for the arson case, I will get Mr Frank Safely on it as soon as I can.

I assume that you do not want Ms. Melody Lime investigated. The Bright Report cannot condone the theft of property – no matter how noble the reason. However, as you have provided scant description of the person, perhaps there is not much to go on.

Please enjoy your vacation.

P.S. Ernest and I would love some pomegranates.

Best regards,
L.F. Balding Jr. III

ENTERTAINMENT: A BOARDGAME STORY
BY NIGEL MEEPLE

The Unboxing

"Another one?" she asked raising that eyebrow.

I explained that it was for work – every boardgame I brought home was for work nowadays.

"That means that it's going back, right? Coz the others are gathering dust like nobody's business."

I – an experienced boyfriend – bit my tongue. The reason the boxes were the exclusive domain of dust bunnies and cobwebs was that my dear Rose only liked to play a particular one. Grant it, it was the best one we owned. Grant it, we were evenly matched. But sometimes…

"Yes," I said. "Only have this one for the weekend, so dust won't have an opportunity to settle."

"Good," she said cheerfully. "Don't forget the party this weekend – and yes, you have to come too – Theodora invited us especially."

I assured her that I had not forgotten – which was the truth, I was dreading it. Several hours of conservative chitchat about how the country had gone downhill. Be that as it may, there was nothing like a fresh boardgame to distract the mind.

I found my favorite table and packed out the box. This board game was called *I Have an Inkling*, a game by an unknown publisher and an unlisted designer. The design on the box was clean and simple: white, with blue lines on it like that of an exam pad. The title was formed from stylized inkblots. The lettering had a slight Rorschach test aesthetic – which made me feel uneasy.

The game – according to the finely printed blurb on the back – was about making it in the world of the written word. The first player to attain immortality – either by selling out to Hollywood or writing an incomprehensible masterpiece – won. The following information applied:

- Playtime: 1 – 72 hours
- Age Range: 21 – 87 years
- Number of Players: 3 – 7

The last requirement gave me pause. It is one of those, I told myself. Usually, when a modern boardgame requires an odd number of players, it implies some 'betrayer' mechanic, or at least, some imbalance of power. Two-player games were challenging to test as it was.

The box rattled as I turned it the right way up again. It seemed to be stuffed with components. I ripped off the plastic and ran my hand over the cardstock box. I love that newly opened boardgame smell – maybe it is just me.

The largest item in the box was the board itself. An array of inkblots, yellowed bits of parchment, and snippets of calligraphy outline an oval route. It reminded me of the popular property buying game we are all familiar with. The notable differences were instead of 'free parking' there was 'free publicity' and instead of 'jail' it had 'literary obscurity'.

Rather than describing each square, I will limit the detail to what crops up in my playthrough. The rest will be for you to discover.

There were hundreds of cards that were to be separated into specific decks. This made it clear that the game was heavily reliant on a deck-building mechanic. This is something that – on its own – I usually find enjoyable. It remains to be seen how this would synergize with the dice-based board movement and the action economy. On the face of it, it all seemed too much.

Along with the standard d6 dice that determined spaces moved per turn, there was an interruption die. The number here was added/subtracted from the first value – unless you rolled a skull. This cost you your turn, signifying a bout of writer's block.

Next was the rulebook. It was a hefty 368-page tome containing not only the rules, but also alternative setups, bits of narrative, and an extensive list of random events (triggered by certain card effects). The thing made an audible thud when it landed on the table.

"Does it come with a story?" asked Rose. There was that raised eyebrow again. "You're never going to finish that in a weekend."

I wanted to disagree, but a growing TBR pile next to the bed would undermine my argument. So, instead, I assured her that I would only follow the 'quick-start' rules for now and only reference specific things as they came up.

Rose cast her eyes over the components. "Looks too complicated," she said. These words gave me a sinking feeling. "You enjoy it," she said. "It is more your thing than mine anyway."

She left me to it and ventured off into her natural hunting grounds: the kitchen. She was not the domestic sort, my Rose – she hated that kind of thing. But when it came to the preparation of food, Rose was something of an athlete. She approached a recipe like a general would battlefield intel. A meal was unworthy of her time unless some element had to rest for an hour, or the recipe had fewer than three pages. She liked rare things – things with unpronounceable names and unlikely flavor combinations. Triumph or flop, it was never simple – never a recipe that a lesser cook would comprehend on a first reading.

I left her to it and returned to my 'over-complicated' boardgame.

I flipped through the rules. I placed the pieces, the score tokens, and the various decks on their allotted spaces. I must make a special mention here that the full setup – at least before play commences – is neat and attractive.

As the game required a minimum of three players, I would have to pretend to have a split personality – again. At least this game did not require an element of charades like my previous review. It is hard to misinterpret yourself on purpose.

However, there was one last thing in the box. It was a 3x3x2 inch metallic block – evidently the source of the box's weight – the epic rulebook notwithstanding. It looked like an external hard drive. Engraved on one side was a code: 'EPAI 2.0'.

It almost seemed out of place – a ray gun amid crackling literary parchment. It required a plug and the Wi-Fi password – things that screamed gimmick in the board game world.

I flipped to the appropriate section in the rules – Fewer Than Two Players – which read:

"In the event that additional players are required – either to meet the minimum requirement of three or to reach the maximum of seven – please make use of the AI unit. Be sure to select the correct product (i.e. *I Have an Inkling*). Results may vary. Use with caution."

This is where I found my first criticism: the power cable was far too short. I ran an extension to the dining room table and waited for the device to charge. I would like to complain about the fact that it had to charge, but this is still better than playing it by myself.

I skimmed through the rules with the background music of clinking crockery. I rolled the dice a few times and delt out the opening hands. The generic cards were beautifully illustrated. Typewriters, quills, inkwells, pens, and sticky-notes represented writing sessions. Each gave the player a certain number of progress and typo points. Progress points brought you closer to completing your current project. Typo points detracted from the overall value of your work and can be negated with Editor cards. As these were the starting cards, they had high typo values and low progress values – representing your inexperience at the start of the game.

Booting up the Players

The holograms took shape – flickering humanoid shapes from the torso up – floating roughly where I told the device the vacant seats were. One was a man with a beret and a pair of tiny spectacles. He reminded me of Mr Bord, except that the apparition was dark skinned and did not have the general air of entitlement about him.

The second was female – cropped hair, sleeveless top, arm dangling over the chairback.

"I am Geffrey Emmerson," said the man. "I am assigned as player two and it will be my honor to outplay you."

"I am Bell Moore," said the woman. "I'll be making the role of player three my own. Watch yourself."

"Pretty cool," said Rose. She walked up to the table and waved a hand through Mr Emmerson. He did not react – evidently the holograms only cared about assigned players. "Amazing technology," said Rose. She kissed me on the cheek. "Enjoy it. Dinner's almost ready."

I dealt out their opening hands (which were read by QR codes hidden in the card backs) and placed out markers on the starting square.

End of Round One

"I complete my novella on the life of a hydrophobic goldfish and gain...four acclaim points," said Geffrey. His hands moved as if he was placing cards on the table. I discarded them on his behalf.

"Totally ridiculous," said Bell crossing her arms. "I can't believe that you justified that premise by saying that a fear of female fish led to his insecurities. One example can't shape his opinion of the gender as a whole."

"Well," said Geffery. "It was a female *piranha* – thank you very much. I was trying to illustrate the dangers of speciesist attitudes and the resulting microaggressions that build self-destructive psychoses. Which disorder do you prefer?"

Bell sneered. "You're completely blind to the gender aspect."

I quietly tallied Geffery's points.

"Yeah, I've got nothing yet," said Bell. She seemed to notice my actions – the level of interactivity was amazing. "Yet," she repeated. "I'm saving up for something big."

They turned to me. There was a moment of stunned silence as I realized that they were waiting for me to say my piece out loud.

"Umm...I'm halfway through a historical fiction novel, but I seem to be stuck in the middle somewhere." I lacked the cards to garner the required number of progression points.

"Amazing," said Geffery. "Which era? Are you taking an original perspective? Are you acknowledging the colonial lens your white maleness dooms you too or...?"

I was taken aback. Feeling slightly insulted and slightly inadequate, I shrugged. "The...the cards don't say."

"Of course they don't," said Bell. She shook her head. "The cards, the dice, the board – all of it – just placeholders. The creative part must come from you. That's the whole point."

"You might as well let it play itself otherwise," said Geffery.

I was starting to get the hang of this.

End of Round Two

Bell's ghostly hand reached for the "complication" deck. I obliged her by turning it over.

"Lo, undetached rabbit parts," she read. "Your work does not mean what you thought it did. Lose three acclaim points. Darn it!"

"Metaphors can only get you so far," said Geffery. "Most readers don't want to do the work of interpretation. It's better to just say it like it is."

"Underestimating the reader's intelligence, are we Geffery? Oh, great literary mind, please tell me how to simplify my work so the common man can understand my lofty ideas," said Bell. She placed the back of her hand against her forehead. "Oh, please. Give me a break! Who writes an adult novel for a first-time reader, huh? People have read other things. They know and understand things. You can't forget that."

"You still lose three acclaim points," said Geffery coolly.

"Yes, I do," she sighed.

They turned to me. I looked over the cards I had played this round. My lofty historical novel on the Napoleonic Wars from Empress Joséphine's perspective was dropped in favor of something lighter.

"I've completed the first four issues of my grimdark graphic novel series. This tallies up to eleven acclaim points."

"Excellent," said Geffery.

"Probably glorifies violence," said Bell rolling her eyes. "And probably oversexualizes and objectifies women."

"And they are probably all white," said Geffery as he wiped his glasses on his cardigan. "They are, aren't they?"

I was ready for this. "No, actually," I said. I cleared my throat. "It's an African take on the Caped Crusader and his companion. They're all women – I even gender-swapped the Rogue's Gallery."

"Let me get this straight," said Bell leaning closer. "You made something your own by simply changing the race and gender? Are you serious?"

I wanted to protest, but…yes, she was right.

"He's going for the 'selling out to Hollywood' victory condition," said Geffery.

"So cheap," said Bell. "Whatever! Take your points, Player One. I guess the game uses the realities of the industry to make it realistically unfair."

I swallowed hard. I could feel my cheeks burning as I moved my score marker up eleven places.

"Your new friends sound really annoying," said Rose. She

appeared in a cloud of kitchen aromas. I was so engrossed in the game that I hardly noticed anything else. "Come on," she said. "Put it away. Dinner's ready."

Mid-Game Break

I struggled to sleep that night. I stared up at the ceiling and listened to Rose snore. My mind wondered back to the game. There was little satisfaction in just playing the cards. You had to argue your point – you had to impress the others. That is where the true fun was hidden.

I drifted off, thinking of fresh takes on literary classics – forgetting that my competition were pre-programmed entities.

The Party

I faded into the background. It was the best strategy for these occasions. While the others 'caught up', I snuck glances at my phone (I had taken sneaky pictures of the manual before we left).

"What are you busy with, Nigel?" someone asked. I dropped my phone into my pocket. "Still writing that book? What was it again?"

"Umm," was the best I could manage.

"He has a *real* job now," said Rose. "Writing for a news journal. Real important stuff."

I managed an awkward nod.

"Still stories, though, right?" asked the friend. I think her name was Emma. "Where do you get your ideas? I mean, some of the things people come up with – am I right? You must be tripping, right?"

"If only it was that simple," I said. "It takes a lot more – "

"Well, Rachelle over there writes vampire YA," probably-Emma continued. "It's really saucy stuff. You should write something like that."

Rose squeezed my arm – the signal for "now-now, be nice".

Probably-Emma looked at me expectantly. I got this a lot. Usually, the best tactic was to nod and change the subject, but she did not wait for my reply.

"Rachelle!" she shouted above the thumping background music. "Come tell Nigel about your stories. He needs some help."

Rose squeezed my arm again.

Rachelle sauntered up, wine in hand, chunky jewelry clinking. There was an exchange of 'whats' as they struggled to hear each other over the throng.

"Oh, right," said Rachelle as she sized me up. "You're probably not into vampire fiction," she said. "You're probably one of those that doesn't see it for the art it really is."

I heard Geffery and Bell's voices in my head. Instead of escaping the situation with a solemn nod, I said: "Amazing. Is yours an original take on the genre?" Rose's grip tightened on my arm. "Are you acknowledging the fact that modern vampire romances are veiled yearnings for traditional – pre-feminist – gender roles where a dangerous male claims a submissive female? Are you mixing it up or…?"

Rachelle and Probably-Emma stared at me for a moment. Rose cut off the circulation to my fingers.

"I think you're trying to insult me," said Rachelle. "What do you know about feminism anyway? You're a man – or so Rose tells us." She drained her glass. "FYI, my book isn't pre-feminist or whatever. My Count Raul is a gentleman. He saves Penelope from the trashy men in her life – from weaklings like you."

The Aftermath

The drive home was quiet.
"Technically, she's the one that got personal," I said.
Silence.
"I was just trying to find out more," I said.
"No, you weren't," said Rose coldly. "You hoped she wouldn't understand your insult."
"Technically, she didn't," I said. I should have bit my tongue.
"*Technically*, you ruined the party," she said. "Don't think we'll be invited to another one for a while. When will we see our friends again?"
"*Your* friends," I said. This killed the conversation for the rest of the night. I was starting to understand why Mr Bord was such a lonely figure.

End of Round Six

"You're not even trying," said Geffery. He flickered above his chair. "A woke version of Robinson Crusoe is such low hanging fruit."

"I don't think someone's done it," said Bell. "That makes it fair game in my book. Besides, I thought you'd like something about reverse-colonialism."

Geffery smiled. "What made you think that? Are you presupposing that I'd like something like that because…?"

"I liked it," I said. They stared at me. "Well, the board likes it too. Bell is four points away from winning."

"I can live with that," said Bell. "And just so you know, Geffery, I'm not presupposing anything. It's based on what you've been asking for all game."

"So now it's fan service?" said Geffery.

"We can't argue about everything," I said.

"Why not?" they asked in unison.

"What's the point of something if you can't pull it apart?" asked Bell. "How will you understand anything then?"

"What if it is wrong or harmful?" asked Geffery. "Are you just going to accept it for the sake of…what? If you leave things be, then they can creep in and hurt you when you least expect it."

"You'll be trapped in a world where other's get to tell you how to think," said Bell.

"But how do you enjoy things then?" I asked.

The holograms exchanged glances.

"I don't entirely understand the question," said Geffery. "Sure, there may be some things that are unforgivably broken, but for the most part there's something great about everything. Something to enjoy."

"I guess he's got a point," said Bell. "Sometimes things are more interesting if you understand all the angles. But that doesn't mean you can let things slide – if you know what I mean."

The Resolution

The final tally was:

1. Bell, *Incomprehensible Master* victory condition, six works complete, the final 2000-page manifesto on the misrepresentation on female animals in animation clinching the required points.

2. Geffery, second place, three points short of the *Jack-of-All-Trades* victory condition, eleven works completed.
3. Me, third place, six points short of the *Selling Out* victory condition, eight works (one of which was 90% typos) complete.

The game took about twenty hours to complete (device charging time not included). It was fun and frustrating. Most of all, I had a knot in my stomach. However, this was probably not entirely due to my third-place finish.

Rose was icing the Apology Cupcakes when I sauntered into the kitchen.

"I'm the one that should apologize," I said. "At least she has a published novel – so who am I to criticize."

"Uh-huh," she said.

She made swirling roses of chocolate icing on each of the cupcakes. I finished it off with sprinkles – adding more here and there at the direction of a silent finger.

"Did you beat your game?" she asked once we finished.

"It beat me," I said. "I quite like it, you know."

"Because of the game or because of the talking?" she asked already knowing the answer.

I helped her pack the cupcakes in the carrier box. "There's a fan club," I said. "In the back of the rulebook, I mean."

"Great," she said. She kissed me on the cheek.

Verdict

I greatly enjoyed *I Have an Inkling*. It is not the best board game I have ever played, but it certainly one that made me reassess things. The systems are highly convoluted and often trip over each other. Some of the cards have minimal impact – making some turns feel wasted. This might contribute to the long playtime and may put off causal players.

True enjoyment comes from the discussions. Without having to defend your inventions in front of a panel of your peers, the game becomes a card milling free-for-all. The best component in the box is the AI device – something I initially wrote off as a gimmick. The realism of the artificial players and their level of interactivity is astounding.

It was the hardest thing to return.
Overall, I give the game a strong **7/10**.

Returning the Box

I made my way back to the factory, deep in thought. I called Rose as I drove. We made plans to see her friends again and I promised to give Rachelle's book a try. I subsequently promised not to tell anyone what I thought about it.

"Maybe you need that fan club," she said. "You can argue all the fiddly stuff there."

I pulled up to the factory. The building was just as unmarked as the box itself. The man in the lab coat that took the board game from me is equally nondescript.

"It all worked properly?" he asked.

"Better than expected," I said.

He shook the box. "A little lighter than I remember. Is the rulebook…?"

"Yeah," I said. "The rulebook is definitely in there."

The man seemed happy with this. We said our goodbyes and I drove home eager to play another game. This time I would not need to misinterpret myself.

EDITOR'S NOTE
MEET THE STAFF OF THE BRIGHT REPORT

The Bright Report has always endeavored to bring its readership unusual stories that highlight the complexities and simplicities of the human condition. We want to make you think – usually, right after we make you feel. Regardless of whether a story is silly or serious (which are not entirely opposites), each one contains a subtle truth about life and the people who live it.

Here is a brief run-down of the Staff of the Bright Report that are featured in this volume. This newsprint is committed to representing a vast array of backgrounds, genders, races, and kinks. (The mention of the latter came at the insistence of Mr Bord.)

Lazen F. Balding Jr. III
Editor-in-Chief of the Bright Report

Yours truly. Former reporter at the Literature Desk. I guide our fearless team by striving to sniff out stories that might have otherwise fallen through the cracks. Plus, with so many strong personalities in one publication, I have the unenviable task of making sure that everyone gets equal billing and credit. What makes it into an edition of the Bright Report (or this volume of 'best of' stories, for that matter) is up to me.

Carmichael Carmichael
Explorer Extraordinaire, Travel Desk

An enigmatic figure and a legend in his own lifetime, Mr Carmichael explores the world with an infectious enthusiasm. Never afraid to get stuck in – whether it is an obscure rain dance performed on a ranch in Midwest United States or a debate on the Fourth Industrial Revolution in the jungles of the Congo – Mr Carmichael is your man. Bringing a misguided western perspective to both the unusual and the familiar, our resident explorer has a unique voice.

Charline Ratanang
Journalist, Sports Desk

Retired icon of women's cricket, Ms. Ratanang now scours the world for a sport she cannot play. She has taken thousands of wickets and hit many a six, but now she wants something that will reignite the fiery spark of competition within her. She not only reports on unusual sporting events but also takes part in them. Highly competitive and highly skilled, Ms. Ratanang likes a good game. Never let her challenge you to a game of darts.

Jacques Bord
Senior Journalist, Literature Desk

Ever wished that you could spend your days sipping something strong, drawing on an expensive cigar, and having a deep conversation with a literary mind? This is the privilege that Mr Bord extends to all his interviewees. No one believes in his abilities to pull a piece of prose apart like Mr Bord does. His name appears on many letters of complaint addressed to the Bright Report – something in which he takes great pride.

Jamison Jefferson Jones
Journalist, Motoring Desk

A world-renowned petrol head who has a strong opinion on every luxury vehicle and supercar ever designed, Mr Jones has a great many skills behind the wheel. Now, in the autumn of his years, he has given up the high-octane world of televised motor mayhem to write pieces for the Bright Report. Now, if only we can bring the cost of his insurance down.

Nigel Meeple
Junior Journalist, Entertainment Desk

The newest member of the team, Mr Meeple has shown great talent. By questioning what others take for granted and by always getting to the humanity of the story at hand, he has shown to have the heart of a journalist. We are watching Mr Meeple's career with great hope and interest.

Pash Tensing
Journalist, Art Desk

Winner of the *What's that Supposed to Be* International Art Award three years in a row, Ms. Tensing has shown great talent with a brush and ruler. She enjoys a measure of precision in her work, which not only affords her with the neatest office at the Bright Report HQ, but also results in the most accurate pieces of journalism we have ever seen. She is the heart of the office, for no space is complete without a complicated Tensing maze piece.

The Late Lady Bright
Founder of the Bright Report

Our founder, Lady Lucina Annamaria Marquez Bright founded the Bright Report after retiring from a life of high adventure. Tired of impersonal and (often) negative stories in mainstream news media, she endeavored to create something new – news that she can read at her leisure – news that left her feeling slightly happier. Sadly, she did not live long enough to see her little publication turn into the institution it is today. She died at the age of eighty-four in a convoluted airship accident.

There are – of course – many more talented writers, journalists, and contributors that write for the Bright Report. I hope, dear reader, that you will join us in the next volume where you will encounter the other bright minds that work here.

Furthermore, if any of the stories contained here in touched you or – alas – offended you, please write to our offices by post, telegram, or carrier pigeon. If these methods are unavailable to you, please use the web address listed under the meta section (labeled *About the Author*) near the back of this volume.

Until then, find a bit of sunshine and look on the bright side.

L.F. Balding Jr. III

EXTRAS

One can find stories anywhere – it is a matter of looking in the right place or looking in the right way. Here are a few tiny stories that made it into the margins of the regular editions of the Bright Report. If these stories develop into something bigger, we will get one of our reporters to do a feature.

Monster in the Highstreet

The Millgate Blob has struck again. This time it was spotted oozing into several high-end fashion boutiques. Spokespeople for these establishments claim that the creature rolled in 'just to have a look'. They claim that the Blob left under persistent pestering from shop assistants asking if it needed any help. More on the Millgate Blob when the monstrosity reappears.

Chrome Ice Cream

Hikers in the Drakensburg in South Africa happened upon a strange sight one morning when they discovered a shining sculpture near the summit of Mafadi. It was shaped like a swirly soft serve ice cream – although the hikers called it something else. It is not known if this is connected to the recent spate of monolith discoveries in Utah, Romania, and beyond.

Mansion Murders

A spate of mansion murders has been reported in the small town of Broadly-on-Kleet. Local police are baffled as to the identity of the culprit. They ask that anyone with information about these occurrences come forward. They believe that the murderer is someone who has access to the servants' quarters, has knowledge of the comings and goings of staff and family, and are well acquainted with the victims.

A Cryptic Message

The Bright Report receives piles of fan mail, complaints, and story tips on a daily basis. This comes with the territory. Be that as it may, we have received several strange messages of late. Our crack team of journalists are trying to decrypt the nonsense in hopes of discovering its true meaning. We have yet to crack it. Therefore, we decided to print the latest message here, in hopes that one of our readers might solve it.

The message reads as follows:

EHRFS DGDMR WQTUL KHQUW DEDII VFFZP AWVJI

PDKXU PJDRH AQKVE WCMZS NYFKH DZMFD HMRAJ

KAKME MFIGM VVLZF FHRVU DXHMI ASRYL DIZYC JPGXY

FZQNI DPMOD IAXNE HZRGK UCGWL RDIUL CAVWI UVSXW

GDNFS NFPPY GMYMG FLCSY FHKAF MBJFP EQQAA VQCJY

EUMVM NWLTE FUCMI XNQSV ESAIZ XODDI HMBHA VGKFE

DCAYA BKCJI SPGEG EQPOY XOVCJ UJQGC COARR NNWQR

PHOOP NDKUY HCRPW PWMAD EHDZL VGBCW QISPK IKNOJ

X

Please write to us if you have figured it out.

Pet Health

Is your artificially engineered giant tardigrade mentally healthy? A new manual by self-styled moss-piglet guru, Sonya Loopington suggests seven ways of psychically determining the mood of your eight-legged darling in her new book, *Tardy to Tardigreat!* The Bright Report's own Jacques Bord wrote in his review: *They have done worse things to paper – I am sure they must have. But this is up there. This book made me laugh and cry. The latter was because there are only so many hours in a man's life.*

Missing Magic Formula

A contact within Flamingo Industries has informed the Bright Report that the formula for the company's new energy drink has gone missing. The *Booster Ten Thousand Plus One* was said to launch next summer. With the formula stolen, it seems likely that the multimillion-dollar launch will have to be postponed. Flamingo Industries have yet to confirm this development. Our contact alleged that this was corporate espionage perpetrated by their competitor, Invocorp. More on this story as it develops.

Kitjovistinope Knits

The latest craze in winter fashion comes in the form of knitted beanies emblazoned with the word 'Kitjovistinope'. These multihued hats have become the symbol of tolerance in popular culture. While other movements have dubious flags, banners, and baseball caps, the *Kitjovistinope Marchers* – as they have dubbed themselves – have taken this word to heart. They march in defense of those who try everything to get by. This movement welcomes those of every color, creed, religion, gender identity, and dietary preference. They urge those who feel that *'everyone should just get along'* to don such a beanie to show their support.

Coming Soon

In the next volume:

- **Mr Stanswobble** is on the trail of a rock band on a mission in *Murky Dishwater and the Quest for Peace.*

- **Ms. Dumont** explores the world of bespoke cheese rolling in *Double Gloucester and the Question of Provenance.*

- **Mme Geist** investigates the strange sightings of a creature in a small town in *Cryptid Squatter's Rights.*

- The continuation of **Mr Carmichael's** adventure in the Cloud Islands.

- And many more…

Hopefully, we will find out what happened to **Ms. Shánzé** from the political desk by the next volume.
 Also, Mr Carmichael's assistant – **Ms. Bly** – has gone missing. Anyone with any information about a lost explorer, please contact us as soon as possible. Ms. Bly is described as feisty, determined, and fearless by her mentor. She was last seen commandeering an icebreaker headed for the Arctic Circle.

The Bright Report
EST · 1921

ABOUT THE AUTHOR

People describe Marcel M du Plessis as anything but the *'quiet type'*. The closest he gets to it is during the dark brooding moods – during which he writes stories of horror, political intrigue, and tragedy. The rest of the time he will talk your head off about something nerdy or try to make you laugh with a funny story he made up. He attempted to do the latter here in hopes that he will build a readership that will become comfortable with his comedy before he breaks their hearts with his other fiction.

If you would like to become part of a community of fans, go to:

www.calliopesprisoner.co.uk

OTHER TITLES BY THE AUTHOR

Awkward Phrasing

An introduction to the Bright Report. Introduces some of the journalists who work at the journal will giving a brief tour of the HQ.

The Bright Report Volume 2

The second volume of the Bright Report contains the following stories:

- Murky Dishwater, an unusual rock band with an unusual sound - what is their secret?
- Cheese rolling is a dangerous business, but did you know that the cheese goes through several 'hill tests' before it can carry the name of Double Gloucester?
- An apartment full of unusual creatures asserts their right to squat where they want to.
- An unusual writing implement is said to bring the wielder great literary success, but at what cost?
- Mr Carmichael washes up on a strange island where the residents sort themselves into the Likins and the Knopes.

The Silent Symphony

Cassius Wortham leaves all he knows behind to make it as a writer in the City, a nameless, walled metropolis at the crossroads of the world. But things are not as they seem. His roommate might have mob connections, his artist friend has addiction issues, and the waitress at the poetry club has political aspirations. Not to mention the invisible spirit of history that follows them around waiting to chronicle a looming catastrophe. An overseas turmoil brings tides of refugees to the walls of the City. Ambitious leaders play at social engineering. The loudest voices are drowned in the growing silence. Only Cas, his friends and their ghostly tagalong hold the key to the future, for in the end the Silent will decide the fate of the City. Listen…and you too may hear the instruments of the Silent Symphony.

Can you find all the secrets? Can you find the truth? Do you know why the City fell?

This page was left blank by accident.
(While you're here, please consider leaving a review on the Amazon or Goodreads page – this would really help me).

Printed in Great Britain
by Amazon